To Carol

In memory of our New York visit.

Carol

The fox thought his paw was cut and ran away.
See page 130.

UNCLE WIGGILY
ON THE FARM

By
HOWARD R. GARIS

AUTHOR OF

Uncle Wiggily's Airship; Uncle Wiggily's
Automobile; Uncle Wiggily's Travels; Uncle
Wiggily's Story Book

ILLUSTRATED BY ELMER RACHE

UNCLE WIGGILY
Reg. U. S. Pat. Off:

·NEW·YORK·
·THE·PLATT·&·MUNK·Co·INC·

PUBLISHERS NOTE

The stories herein contained appeared originally in the Evening News, of Newark, N. J., where (so many children and their parents have been kind enough to say) they gave pleasure to a number of little folks and grown-ups also. Permission to issue the stories in book form was kindly granted by the publisher and editor of the News, to whom the author extends his thanks.

CONTENTS

STORY I

UNCLE WIGGILY AND THE OATS

Uncle Wiggily Longears, the nice bunny rabbit gentleman who lived in Woodland, was not very well.

"I think you had better call Dr. Possum," said Uncle Wiggily to Nurse Jane Fuzzy Wuzzy, his muskrat lady housekeeper. "Perhaps he can make me feel better."

In came Dr. Possum, with his satchel of medicine hanging over his back from the crook in his tail, just as the little possums cling to their mother's tail when they go out with her looking for something to eat.

"I don't feel at all good, Dr. Possum," said Uncle Wiggily.

"Ho! Hum! Let me look at your tongue," said the animal doctor.

And when Uncle Wiggily had stuck out his tongue, and it had been looked at—both sides— the bunny said:

"What kind of medicine are you going to give me, Dr. Possum?"

"No medicine at all!" said Dr. Possum. "What

you need is to get out in the country, breathe
fresh air and eat lots of lettuce and turnips and
cabbage and milk. Get out in the country on a
farm!"

"On a farm!" cried Uncle Wiggily.

"Yes, on a farm," spoke Dr. Possum again.
"Go live on a farm—you and Nurse Jane. It
will do you both good."

Uncle Wiggily twinkled his pink nose once or
twice, like a raisin in the middle of a sugar cookie,
and then he said:

"Well, I think it would be nice on a farm.
Come on, Nurse Jane, we'll go!"

And before another week had passed Uncle
Wiggily and Nurse Jane Fuzzy Wuzzy were
living in a hollow stump bungalow on a nice
farm that the bunny uncle had bought. It was
not far from where Sammie and Susie Littletail,
the rabbit children lived, nor was it a great way
from the trees where Johnnie and Billie Bushytail the squirrel boys scampered about.

And, as I have told you, in other books, many
stories about Uncle Wiggily finding his fortune,
and having adventures, and going to the seashore,
up in an airship and riding in an automobile, now
I will tell you some stories that happened him
when he was on his farm.

And now to begin:

"I shall be very busy today, Nurse Jane," spoke Uncle Wiggily as he slowly walked off the porch of his hollow stump farm house. "Very busy, indeed, I shall be. In fact you might put me up a little lunch to take with me."

"A lunch? Oh, Wiggy! Why?" she asked. "Aren't you coming home to lunch?"

"I don't believe I'll have time," answered the rabbit gentleman. "You see, I have to go and call on many of my friends."

"Aren't you going to attend to your farm?" the muskrat lady asked.

"Oh, yes, and it is about my farm that I go to call on the other animal folk. You see the oats on my farm are getting ripe and ready to cut. I need help, as there are so many oats, and I am going around to ask Sammie and Susie Littletail, the rabbits; Johnnie and Billie Bushytail, the squirrels; Jackie and Peetie Bow-wow, the puppy dog boys, and all my other big and little friends to come and help gather the oats. That is why I will not be back to lunch."

"Then I'll put you up a nice one," said Nurse Jane.

In a basket she put some lettuce sandwiches with slices of carrot between them. There were also some watermelon seed, ice cream puffs and a little cabbage jelly spread over cucumber bread.

Oh, it was a very fine lunch, indeed, and makes me hungry when I write about it.

So, with his lunch in a basket over his paw, off started the bunny uncle to ask his friends to come and help him gather the oats that grew on his farm.

"Come and help you? Of course we will!" cried all the animal folk, big and little. For they loved Uncle Wiggily and wanted to do him a favor.

Over to the oat field they went, and then such a busy time as there was!

The rabbits and the squirrels, also the doggies, bit off the oat stalks with their sharp teeth. The ducks, Lulu, Alice and Jimmie Wibblewobble, and Grandfather Goosey Gander, nibbled off the oats in their bills. And Neddie and Beckie Stub-tail, the kind bears, pulled them off with their claws.

"My! I'll certainly have a lot of oats this year!" cried Uncle Wiggily, making his pink nose twinkle as he stood in the field and watched the grain being gathered. "There'll be enough for Gup, the kind old horse, as well as for the ponies, Dottie and Munchie Trot. It is very good of you, my friends, to help me gather the oats."

"Oh, we like it!" cried Sammie Littletail. "It is like a picnic to us."

"It would be a real picnic if there was something to eat and some pink lemonade to drink," spoke Alice Wibblewobble.

"Bless your wing feathers!" cried Uncle Wiggily. "Of course, there's something to eat."

And then, surely enough, along came Nurse Jane Fuzzy Wuzzy and Old Mother Goose, bringing a number of baskets filled with good things from peanuts to ice-cream-popcorn-balls.

When all the oats were cut down the animal folk gathered together and carried them into Uncle Wiggily's barn. There they were put in a big box or bin, like the coal bin, only it was made of white, clean boards, and not black and dirty ones.

"Well, I think I'll go out in the barn and look at my oats," said Uncle Wiggily, about a week after they had been stored in the bin. "I want to see if I have room for any more."

So out to the barn went the bunny uncle, and, climbing to the top of the oat bin, or box, he looked down inside. But something must have happened, for all of a sudden Uncle Wiggily's paw slipped, and right down among the oats he fell head over heels.

The oats were almost as soft as hay, so he did

not get hurt in the least, but when he tried to walk across them and to the edge of the bin he sank down almost to his shoulders. The oats were soft and shiny-slippery, and it was like trying to climb up a hill of sliding sand. Uncle Wiggily could not do it.

"Oh, dear!" he cried, his pink nose twinkling like a looking glass in summer. "I'll never get out of here. I'll have to stay in the oat bin forever! Oh, dear!"

He tried and tried again to get up the slippery hill of oats in the bin, but he could not. Then he cried:

"Help! Help! Will no one help me?"

"Why, yes, I'll help you. Who are you and where are you? a voice outside the barn asked.

"I'm in the oat bin! Please get me out," answered the bunny gentleman.

Into the barn came running Neddie Stubtail, the little boy bear. He was just passing and had heard Uncle Wiggily call.

"I can't see you," said Neddie, as he stood in the middle of the barn floor.

"Well, I'm inside the bin, and it's so slippery I can't get out," said Uncle Wiggily. "But there is a hole in the bottom of the bin, through which the oats slide out. The hole is covered by a board. Pull out this board and I will slide out with the oats."

Neddie the boy bear did this. Out came sliding the slippery oats through the hole just as coal slides out of the wagon. And with the oats out on the barn floor shot Uncle Wiggily, not hurt a bit but a little dusty and quite sneezy, for the dust from the oats got up his nose.

"Thank-ker-snit-zio-you, Ned-ager-choo-die," he said, and Neddie laughed.

So that's how the bunny gentleman fell into the oats and got out again, and if the sweet pickle doesn't fall into the barrel of sauerkraut and get its warts so mussed up it can't go to the clam chowder party I'll tell you next about Uncle Wiggily and the cows.

STORY II

UNCLE WIGGILY AND THE COWS

"Uncle Wiggily, are you going to take a hop over your farm this morning?" asked Susie Littletail, the rabbit girl, as she walked up the front steps of the bunny gentleman's hollow stump farm house, where he was sitting on the porch.

"Why, yes, Susie, I generally take a walk over my farm every day, to see how the things are growing," he said. "Why did you ask me?"

"Because I'd like to go with you this time," answered the little rabbit lassie. "Some day I may want to live on a farm myself and it would be a good thing for me to know all about it."

"Indeed it would," Uncle Wiggily agreed. "There are many things to learn about a farm. I feel better since I came to live in the country on a farm. I'll be happy and pleased if you will come along with me."

"And maybe we'll have an adventure," laughed Susie.

"Maybe we shall. I hope so," Uncle Wiggily cried, making his pink nose twinkle so that it looked almost like a strawberry tart. "I haven't

had an adventure in some time. Come along,
Susie."

So the bunny gentleman and the rabbit girl
went along together, paw in paw, over the farm.
Uncle Wiggily showed Susie where the lettuce
was growing, where the carrots kept their yellow pointed bodies hidden under the brown earth
until it was time for them to be pulled, and many
other things growing on his farm did the bunny
uncle show to Susie.

All of a sudden, as they were looking to see if
the pop corn had made itself into baseballs, Susie
gave a cry.

"Oh, Uncle Wiggily! Look at that big
spider!" exclaimed the little rabbit girl. "I'm
afraid it will bite me. It's bigger than the one
that sat down beside Miss Muffet. Oh, dear."

"Where is the spider?" asked the bunny gentleman, peering through his glasses.

"There!" and Susie pointed to a fence rail on
which something was crawling.

"It is a big one," said Uncle Wiggily. "But I
guess it won't hurt you, Susie."

"Indeed, and I will not," the crawling creature
said. "Besides, I'm not a spider."

"Indeed!" spoke Mr. Longears, politely. "But
you look like a spider and crawl like one."

"Well, perhaps I am a sort of spider," said the

crawling chap, "but I do not spin a web. I am
Daddy Longlegs. That's who I am."

"Oh, I've heard about you," said Uncle Wiggily. "I'm sorry Susie made a fuss about you."

"Oh, that's all right," said the Daddy Longlegs, kindly. "I'm used to little girls screaming
when they see me, for I do look a little like a
spider, though I would never harm anyone."

"I'm sure you would not," the bunny uncle
said. "You may stay on my farm as long as you
like and crawl all over my fences."

"Thank you," the Daddy Longlegs replied.
"You have been kind to me, and it is not often
anyone acts that way toward me. If ever I can
do you, or any of your friends, a favor, I shall
be very pleased to."

"Pray do not mention it," spoke Uncle Wiggily, politely.

"How could a Daddy Longlegs do a favor?"
asked Susie, as she and the bunny uncle went on
again over the farm.

"You never can tell," said Mr. Longears.
"Stranger things have happened. Let us wait
and see."

Pretty soon they came to where Uncle Wiggily was growing some strawberries, and the ripe
red fruit looked so nice that Susie and Uncle
Wiggily stopped to pick some to eat.

"I must come over here soon and get enough
for Nurse Jane to make into a shortcake," said
the rabbit gentleman, as he and Susie walked on.

They had not hopped very far before, all of a
sudden, they heard a sad voice saying:

"Oh, dear! I'll never find them, I know I
won't! Oh, dear, I don't see what they wanted to
hide away from me for, just when I'm in such a
hurry. It's too bad!"

"That sounds like trouble, "said Uncle Wiggily.

"It surely does," agreed Susie. "I wonder
who it is?"

Just then, through the bushes, came bursting
Jackie Bow Wow, the little puppy dog boy.

"Oh Uncle Wiggily—Susie!" he cried. "Have
you seen them?"

"What?" asked the bunny uncle.

"Mother Goose's cows," was the answer. "She
sent me to find them in the fields near your farm,
but the cows aren't here. I can't find them any-
where, and I'm in a hurry to get back to play ball
with the boys."

"We'll help you find the cows," said Uncle
Wiggily, and he and Suise looked also. But no
cows could they find, and Jackie was getting
more and more anxious.

"What seems to be the trouble?" asked a voice,

and there, on the fence rail, sat Daddy Long-legs.

"I can't find the cows," said Jackie.

"Look over there," spoke Daddy, pointing one of his longs legs. "The cows are in those bushes," and, surely enough, they were.

"How did you know they were there?" asked Jackie, as he barked and drove the cows home to Mother Goose to be milked.

"Oh, we Daddy Longlegs always show where the lost cows are," was the answer. "That's what we're for."

"Thank you, very much," said Uncle Wiggily. "You see, Susie, the Daddy Longlegs did do a favor after all."

"I see," said Susie, and then she went on home over the farm fields with Uncle Wiggily, while Daddy Longlegs crawled on the fence looking for more lost cows.

And, if the table legs don't step in the milk pitcher by mistake and get so tangled up they can't dance with the napkin rings, I'll tell you next about Uncle Wiggily and the rake.

STORY III

UNCLE WIGGILY AND THE RAKE

"Where are you going this morning Uncle Wiggily?" asked Nurse Jane Fuzzy Wuzzy, the muskrat lady housekeeper, as she saw the bunny gentleman standing on the front porch of his hollow stump home, looking across his farm. "Are you going to look for any more lost cows?"

"Not this morning," answered the rabbit. "I am going to pull some weeds from where they are growing among my carrots. I can't have the weeds in there."

"Why not?" asked Nurse Jane. "Aren't weeds good?"

"Well, some folks like them almost as much as they do flowers," spoke Mr. Longears, "but I would rather have the weeds out of my garden than in, so I am going to pull them out!"

"How?" asked the muskrat lady.

"With this rake," answered the bunny uncle, and he held up a long-handled thing, on the end of which was a piece of scratchy iron, made with sharp teeth. "The teeth of the rake will pull out the weeds," said Mr. Longears, and, with a hop,

21

skip and jump, over towards the bed of carrots
he started.

On the way be looked at the other things growing on his farm, and he made up his mind that he
would soon have to hoe the dirt up into little hills
around the bean plants, so they would become
larger and stronger.

When he reached the place where the carrots
were growing, Uncle Wiggily began scratching
up the ground with the sharp teeth of the rake,
pulling out the weeds from between the rows of
the vegetables.   And when he stopped to rest he
heard a voice asking him:

"Oh, Uncle Wiggily!   May we take your rake
for a little while?"

The bunny uncle turned in surprise, thinking
perhaps it was some bad creature, like the skillery, scalery alligator, playing a trick on him,
but he only saw Jimmie Wibblewobble, the boy
duck, and with him was Jollie Longtail, the little
mouse boy.

"What do you want of my rake for?" asked
Uncle Wiggily.

"To get our baseball bat down out of a tree,"
spoke Jollie, the mousie chap.

"How did your bat get up in a tree?" the bunny uncle wanted to know.

"We threw the bat up to knock the ball," said

Jimmie. "You see it was this way. We were playing ball and Billie Wagtail, the goat, knocked the ball over the fence and into a tree.. There the ball stuck. To get it down Jackie Bow-Wow threw the bat up at it."

"And the ball came down, but the bat stayed up!" chattered Johnnie Bushytail, the boy squirrel, as he scampered along with his brother Billie and Sammie Littletail, the rabbit chap.

"So we want your rake to pull the bat down out of the tree," said Neddie Stubtail, the little boy bear.

"Take my rake with pleasure," said Uncle Wiggily. "I'll wait here in the shade of this pie-plant until you come back," and he sat down under the broad, green leaves, of the rhubarb or pie-plant, which made a nice shelter from the sun.

Along the ground Neddie dragged the rake, making long, deep scratches in the dirt with the iron teeth.

Pretty soon the animal boys came to the tree where their baseball bat was caught between two branches. The little boy bear, with Billie Wagtail to help him, lifted the rake up in the air, pushed it in among the green leaves, and, when it was caught on a branch, they jiggled it and joggled it, and down came the bat, which is a

round stick of wood that animal chaps and other
boys use to hit the ball.

"Ouch!" cried Jollie Longtail, for the bat fell
on his toes.

"Now let's take Uncle Wiggily's rake back
to him," said Johnnie Bushytail. "I'll do it, as
it isn't my turn to play for a while yet."

So the squirrel chap dragged the rake back
to where Uncle Wiggily was waiting under the
pie-plant. And when Johnnie was almost there,
he heard a rustling in the bushes and a voice
growled:

"Ha! I'll get that rabbit sure, now!
Burr-r-r-r!"

Johnnie looked, and there, creeping toward the
bunny uncle, was the bad old ear-scratching cat.
Johnnie was wondering how he could best tell Mr.
Longears to jump up and run away, when suddenly he saw the creeping cat stop, and look
down at something on the ground.

"Oh my!" yowled the cat. "Some other
scratching creature has been here ahead of me!
Oh, what big deep scratches its claws have made
in the ground. Maybe that scratchy creature
is a friend of Uncle Wiggily's, and if it is—well
it could scratch me all to pieces with such big
claws as it has! Oh, dear! I guess I'll run
away." And, with a last look at the scratches

in the ground, away ran the bad cat, not bothering Uncle Wiggily at all.

"Ho! Ho!" laughed Johnnie as he went on
toward the bunny gentleman. "The cat saw
the scratches made in the ground by the rake,
when Neddie and I dragged it along, and the
cat thought the scratches were made by some big
animal. Ha! Ha! That cat was fooled all
right! But I'm glad, for Uncle Wiggily was
saved."

The bunny uncle was glad, also, for he didn't
like his ears scratched, and, if the sharp church
steeple doesn't make a hole in the rag doll's balloon, so that it bursts and scares the polly-par-
rot, I'll tell you next about Uncle Wiggily and
the hoe.

STORY IV

UNCLE WIGGILY AND THE HOE

"Do you want me to go to the store for you
or do anything like that?" asked Uncle Wiggily
Longears, the rabbit gentleman, as he waved his
wiskers in a good-by to Nurse Jane Fuzzy
Wuzzy, his muskrat lady housekeeper, one morning. He was just going down the front steps of
his hollow stump farm house. "Do you want
anything, Nurse Jane?"

"Where are you going?" she asked.

"Over to my farm bean-patch to hoe up the dirt
around the vines into little hills."

"Are the beans going to slide down hill?" the
muskrat lady wanted to know.

"Ha! Ha!" laughed Uncle Wiggily. "The
beans slide down hill! Ho! Ho! That's pretty
good. No, beans don't do that, Janie. But I
must hoe the dirt into little hills around the vines
so the beans will grow big and strong. With the
dirt hoed into little hills the roots of the beans
will be better covered. But do you want anything?"

"Well, if you get time you might go to the five

and ten cent store and bring me a spool of thread," said Nurse Jane.

"I'll do it," promised Uncle Wiggily. "When I feel like taking a rest from hoeing the beans I'll go to the store for you."

So, with his long-handled hoe over his shoulder, away started the bunny uncle across his farm. His hoe was like a rake, only it had no teeth in it. It pulled the earth together instead of scratching it apart.

Uncle Wiggily went along over his farm, looking on this side and that for the tail-pulling chimpanzee-monkey, or for the ear-scratching cat, but he saw neither of them, and he was glad. Safely he reached his bean-patch, and began to hoe the dirt up into little hills.

"Well, now I think I'll rest awhile, and go to the five and ten cent store for Nurse Jane," said Uncle Wiggily to himself after a bit. "There are not many more bean-hills to make. I can do them when I come back."

Standing the hoe up against the fence, the rabbit gentleman went on to the store, where he asked for a spool of thread.

"What color does Nurse Jane want?" the little mousie girl clerk behind the five and ten cent store counter wanted to know.

"What color?" asked Uncle Wiggily, sort of

puzzled like. "Is there more than one color thread?"

"Of course there is," laughed the mousie girl. "There is red, blue, green, purple, pink, black, white, yellow, scarlet, brown mauve, gray, speckled, spotted—"

"Stop! stop, please!" begged Uncle Wiggily, putting his paws over his ears. "I did not know there was that much thread in the world. Nurse Jane didn't say what color she wanted, so give me a spool of each, and she can take her choice."

So Uncle Wiggily, with forty-leven spools of different colored, spotted, streaked and striped thread in a bundle, started back to his farm, to finish hoeing the beans. And when he got there he saw something that made him feel sad.

For there, in the bean patch, was the bad old tail-pulling monkey, smiling so as to show his teeth.

"I thought you'd come back," said the monkey. "So I waited for you."

"You needn't have troubled yourself," spoke the bunny uncle, unhappy like.

"Oh, don't worry about me, I didn't mind waiting. It was no trouble at all, I assure you. I s'pose you know why I'm here?" asked the monkey.

"Are you going to pull my tail?" asked the rabbit.

"You have guessed it," said the monkey. "I am going to pull your tail! The last time you got away from me, and I haven't pulled a tail in ever and ever so long. I must pull a tail now."

"Then why not pull your own?" asked Uncle Wiggily. "It is much longer, and easier to pull than mine."

"Don't talk nonsense!" exclaimed the monkey chap. "I never pull my own tail. Get ready now, I'm going to pull yours!" and he jumped over to the bunny.

Uncle Wiggily thought for a minute. Then he said:

"Before you pull my tail would you mind letting me hoe the dirt around some more hills of my beans?"

"Yes, you can do that," agreed the monk, as I call him for short. "But be quick about it," and he sat down on the ground near Uncle Wiggily, with his long curly tail stretched out behind him —the monkey's tail, I mean.

Uncle Wiggily began hoeing the dirt, but, instead of making a hill around his beans he slyly hoed a big hill of dirt right over the monkey's tail. A great, big pile of dirt the bunny uncle quickly hoed over the monkey's tail, working very fast.

"There!" suddenly cried Uncle Wiggily, catching up the spools of thread and his hoe, and running away. "Now let's see you chase after me and pull my tail!"

And the bad monkey could not. The pile of dirt on his tail was so heavy that it held him fast and he could not move, and he had to stay there until the rain came and washed away the earth. But Uncle Wiggily got safely home with the thread, and it was a green spool Nurse Jane wanted. All the others of the forty-ten left over she sent back.

So it is a good thing Uncle Wigily, the farmer, had a hoe, and if the board walk doesn't run away with the lemon squeezer and make the nutmeg grater cry, you shall next hear of Uncle Wiggily and the wheelbarrow.

STORY V

UNCLE WIGGILY AND THE WHEELBARROW

"Well, you certainly look as though you were going to be busy today," spoke Nurse Jane Fuzzy Wuzzy, the muskrat lady, as she came out on the front porch of the hollow stump farm house, and looked at Uncle Wiggily, the farmer bunny gentleman. "What are you going to do with that?" she asked.

For the bunny man had a wheelbarrow in front of him and he was wheeling and rolling it along on the grass.

"I'm going over to the far end of my farm," he said, "and wheelbarrow some stones off it. There are so many stones on the ground that nothing will grow.

"I am going to gather them up in a big pile and then, with my wheelbarrow I will cart them over to the river and throw them in. Stones would just as soon be in the water as on land, and I'd a good deal rather have them off my farm. So here I go! Good-bye, Nurse Jane!"

"Good-bye!" called the muskrat lady housekeeper.

Uncle Wiggily went along over the fields and

through the woods, for there were nice woods on
his farm, and, pretty soon, he came to the place
where the ground was covered with stones. Big
stones there were, and little ones, round stones
and square, and some with three corners to them.
Some looked like funny faces, and others like
marbles, or tops or even rag dolls.

"But, no matter how they look, they must get
off my farm," said Uncle Wiggily to himself, and
he began gathering the stones in piles to wheel
away to the river. He had not been working very
long before he heard a cute little voice calling:

"Oh, Arabella! There's Uncle Wiggily! Now
we can have some fun! Come on!"

The bunny gentleman stopped picking up the
stones and looked around. He saw Arabella
Chick and Susie Littletail, the bunny girl. Arabella was a little hen, as you all know. And the
two animal girls had their dolls with them.

"Oh, Uncle Wiggily!" cried Susie. "May we
help you pick up stones?"

"Oh, yes, I guess so," answered the old rabbit
gentleman, good-natured like and jolly.

"And our dolls will help, too," went on Arabella. "Now, Esmeralda Chocolate Spicecake,"
she said to her doll, "you must be real nice and
help Uncle Wiggily pick up the stones."

"And so must you," Clarissa Janet Hummingbird," said Susie to her doll, who had a rubber nose. "Now we'll begin."

So the two little animal girls with their dolls started to help Uncle Wiggily pick up stones for the wheelbarrow. But, bless your hearts, and also your lollypops! Susie and Arabella could only pick up the very littlest stones, especially Arabella, the hen girl, for she had to hold them in her bill.

In her claw she held her doll, Esmeralda Chocolate Spicecake, and Arabella pretended that the doll picked up stones, too, but it was only make-believe. It was the same way with Susie's doll, Clarissa Janet Hummingbird. She could not pick up stones by herself, and the little bunny girl had to do it for her.

And with this, that and the other, and with getting in Uncle Wiggily's way, and picking up little stones and dropping them, and giggling and looking after their dolls, Arabella and Susie did not help the rabbit gentleman quite as much as they thought they were doing.

But, bless your ice cream cones this time, Uncle Wiggily wouldn't make them feel badly by telling the little animal girls they were bothering him. Instead he just gave a jolly laugh and whistle and said:

"Come, now! How would you like a ride in the wheelbarrow?"

"Oh, that will be lovely!" cried Susie.

"And may we take our dolls?" asked Arabella.

"Yes," said Uncle Wiggily.

So into the wheelbarrow jumped the bunny girl and the chicken girl, and Uncle Wiggily gave them and their dolls a nice ride. And then Susie and Arabella thought of something else to play, so away they ran, leaving Mr. Longears to do this farm work in peace. He got rid of them most politely, you see.

Uncle Wiggily was piling up the stones and carting them in the wheelbarrow down to the river, when, all of a sudden, a harsh voice cried:

"Well, you may stop working now, Uncle Wiggily."

"Stop working? Why?" asked the bunny.

"Because I am going to take you off to my den," went on the voice, and out from behind a rock popped the bad fox. "Off to my den you must go, you must go, you must go! Off to my den you must go, my fat rabbit!" he sang, to the tune of London Bridge, and he grabbed hold of Uncle Wiggily.

"Come now!" the fox went on. "I may as well ride to my den in your wheelbarrow, as you rode

Susie and Arabella. I don't like walking, so you must wheel me."

"Very well," spoke Uncle Wiggily sad like and resigned. "Get in and I'll wheel you to your den."

So the fox got into the wheelbarrow, and off started the bunny. But do you s'pose he went to the den of the fox? Indeed he did not. When Uncle Wiggily came to the river bank, where he had been dumping the stones, he suddenly upset the wheelbarrow, fox and all and "plunk!" right into the water splashed the bad creature.

"Oh, wow! Oh, slosh! Oh, slush!" gurgled the fox, making a dreadful fuss, and by the time he swam out, Uncle Wiggily was safely home. So you see, a wheelbarrow is sometimes better than a trolley car. And, if the cocoanut cake doesn't turn into a straw hat for the elephant to sit on when he goes to the moving pictures, I'll tell you next about Uncle Wiggily and the dandelions.

STORY VI

UNCLE WIGGILY AND THE DANDELIONS

"Well! Well! Well!" exclaimed Uncle Wiggily Longears, the rabbit gentleman farmer, one day, as he climbed over the fence and looked down at the ground on part of his farm. "This must never be. Never! I'll have to do something right away about this."

He hurried back to his hollow stump house and took down the hoe and rake that hung out in the woodshed. He was quite excited and flustered, which means kerslostrated, and Nurse Jane Fuzzy Wuzzy, the muskrat lady housekeeper, seeing the bunny gentleman, asked:

"Why, Wiggy! whatever is the matter?"

"Matter? Matter enough!" he answered. "I was just over to the northeast corner of my farm, where I have planted some turnips, and what do you suppose has happened to them?"

"They didn't run away to go see a moving picture show; did they?" inquired Nurse Jane, guessing like.

"No," answered Uncle Wiggily, putting his hoe and rake over his shoulder. "No, not exactly."

"The bad skillery-scalery alligator didn't pull up your turnips, did he?"

"No, but where the turnips ought to be coming up a whole lot of yellow dandelion flowers and weeds have grown. The dandelions fill the ground so full that there is no place for my vegetables. This must never be. I'm going to hoe up and rake up all those yellow flowers, so they won't be in the way of the turnips."

"Well, I s'pose that's the only thing to do," said the muskrat lady, "but still dandelions are pretty."

"Not when they grow in my turnip bed!" exclaimed the bunny uncle. And then, tying his whiskers in a knot so they wouldn't get in his way, he hurried back to that part of his farm where the dandelions were growing in the turnip bed.

"I'll dig them out—every last one of them!" said Mr. Longears to himself. "The idea of those bold dandelions daring to come in my turnip bed. Bur-r-r-r," and Uncle Wiggily shook his head quite savage like; pretending to be very cross and angry, but really he wasn't.

On and on he went, stopping now and then to see how his beans and peas and corn were growing, for on his farm Uncle Wiggily raised many things that are good to eat. As he climbed over the fence, just before he came to the turnip field, he saw, growing down in a corner, one lone, little yellow dandelion flower.

"Ha! One of those bold fellows here, too!" exclaimed the bunny man. "Well, I'll not dig you up, for, as you are alone, you can do no harm. But I'll dig up all the others so they can't grow any more."

The lone little dandelion heard Uncle Wiggily say this and the yellow flower shivered.

"Oh, if I could only grow big and tall, and have legs, so I might go and tell my brothers and sisters what is going to happen to them," the dandelion thought to himself. "But I can't warn them to get away. They will all be killed."

Uncle Wiggily was soon at the field where the dandelions were growing in place of the turnips. Laying down the rake the old rabbit gentleman took his hoe and was just going to dig up a whole clump of the yellow weed-flowers, when a voice behind him said:

"One moment, please!"

"Eh? What's that?" asked Uncle Wiggily.

"Just stop what you are doing and come with me," went on the voice, and there stood the bad old ear-scratching cat, with a cocoanut grater in one paw.

"Do you want me?" asked the rabbit.

"I certainly do," yowled the cat. "I'm going

to scratch your ears good this time. Look here!"

With that the unpleasant creature took the co-coanut grater, which was very rough and sharp, and rubbed it up and down on the wooden fence rail. Slivers and chips of wood were scraped off with a rasping, filing sound.

"That's what will happen to your ears," said the cat. "You have fooled me so many times. getting away from me, that never yet have I had the pleasure of scratching your ears. Now it will be all the worse for you. Come along!"

"No, he isn't going!" suddenly said a voice, seeming to come from down on the ground.

"Oh, isn't he?" asked the ear-scratching cat. "Who says Uncle Wiggily isn't coming with me to my home in the dark and dismal woods? Who says so?"

"I do!" cried a brave voice. "I do!"

"And who are you?" asked the cat.

"The dandy lion!" was the answer. "We are all dandy lions here, and if you don't let Uncle Wiggily alone we'll bite and scratch you and pull your tail—and—and—and—now you just— SCAT!" cried the dandelion flower.

And with that some of the brave "dandy lion" blossoms that had gone to seed blew their fluffy white stuff in the cat's face and made him sneeze and turn a somersault, and he ran away without even tickling the bunny, to say nothing of scratching his ears.

"Well! Well! Well!" exclaimed Uncle Wiggily. "The dandelion flowers saved me. I thank you," he said to them, making a low bow. "And you may grow here as long as you like. I'll never dig you up."

And so the "dandy lions;" or, as most folks call them, dandelions, grew like a patch of sunshine on the bunny gentleman's farm for many years. And if the breakfast roll doesn't tumble off the front stoop and hit the milkman on the nose I'll tell you next about Uncle Wiggily and Lulu's hat.

UNCLE WIGGILY AND LULU'S HAT

"Uncle Wiggily, do you want to do something for me?" asked Nurse Jane Fuzzy Wuzzy, the muskrat lady housekeeper, of the rabbit gentleman one day as he started out from his hollow stump farm house to take a walk in the woods.

"Do something for you, Nurse Jane? Why, of course, I want to," spoke Mr. Longears. "What is it?"

"Just take this piece of pie over to Mrs. Wibblewobble, the duck lady," went on Miss Fuzzy Wuzzy. "I promised to let her taste how I made apple pie out of cabbage leaves."

"And very cleverly you do it, too," said Uncle Wiggily, with a polite bow. "I know, for I have eaten some myself. I will gladly take this pie to Mrs. Wibblewobble," and off through the woods Uncle Wiggily started with it. He did not have to work on his farm that day.

He soon reached the duck lady's house, and Mrs. Wibblewobble was very glad indeed to get the piece of Nurse Jane's pie.

"I'll save a bit for Lulu and Alice, my two little duck girls," said Mrs. Wibblewobble.

"Why, aren't they home?" asked Uncle Wiggily.

"No, Lulu has gone over to a little afternoon party which Nannie Wagtail, the goat girl, is having, and Alice has gone to see Grandfather Goosey Gander. Jimmie is off playing ball with Jackie and Peetie Bow-Wow, the puppy dog boys, so I am home alone."

"I hope you are not lonesome," said Uncle Wiggily.

"Oh, no, thank you," answered the duck lady. "I have too much to do. Thank Nurse Jane for her pie."

"I shall," Uncle Wiggily promised, as he started off through the woods again. He had not gone very far before all of a sudden, he did not stoop low enough as he was hopping under a tree and, the first thing he knew, his tall silk hat was knocked off his head and into a puddle of water.

"Oh, dear!" cried Uncle Wiggily, as he picked up his hat. "I shall never be able to wear it again until it is cleaned and ironed. And how I can have that done out here in the woods is more than I know."

"Ah, but I know," said a voice in a tree overhead.

"Who are you, and what do you know?"

asked the bunny uncle, surprised like and hopeful.

"I know where you can have your silk hat
cleaned and ironed smooth," said the voice. "I
am the tailor bird, and I do those things. Let
me have your hat, Uncle Wiggily, and I'll fix
it for you."

Down flew the kind bird, and Uncle Wiggily
gave her his hat.

"But what shall I wear while I am waiting?"
asked the bunny uncle. "It is too soon for me to
be going about without my hat. I'll need something on my head while you are fixing my silk
stovepipe, dear Tailor Bird."

"Oh, that is easy," said the bird. "Just pick
some of those thick, green leafy ferns and make
yourself a hat of them."

"The very thing!" cried Uncle Wiggily. Then
he fastened some ferns together and easily made
himself a hat that would keep off the sun, if it
would not keep off the rain. But then it wasn't
raining.

"There you are, Uncle Wiggily!" called the
tailor bird at last. "Your silk hat is ready to
wear again."

"Thank you," spoke the bunny uncle, as he
laid aside the ferns, also thanking them. "Now
I am like myself again," and he hopped on

through the woods, wondering whether or not he was to have any more adventures that day.

Mr. Longears had not gone on very much farther before he heard a rustling in the bushes, and then a sorrowful little voice said:

"Oh! dear! How sad! I don't believe I'll go to the party now! All the others would make fun of me. Oh, dear! Oh, dear!"

"Ha! That sounds like trouble!" said the bunny uncle. "I must see what it means."

He looked through the bushes and there, sitting on a log, he saw Lulu Wibblewobble, the little duck girl, who was crying very hard, the tears rolling down her yellow bill.

"Why, Lulu! What's the matter?" asked Uncle Wiggily.

"Oh dear!" answered the little quack-quack child. "I can't go to the party; that's what's the matter."

"Why can't you go?" Uncle Wiggily wanted to know. "I saw your mother, a little while back, and she said you were going."

"I know I was going," spoke Lulu, "but I'm not now, for the wind blew my nice new hat into the puddle of muddy water, and now look at it!" and she held up a very much bedraggled and debraggled hat of lace and straw and ribbons and flowers.

"Oh, dear! That hat is in a sad state, to be sure," said Uncle Wiggily. "But don't cry Lulu. Almost the same thing happened to me and the tailor bird made my hat as good as ever. Mine was all mud, too, like yours. Come, I'll take you to the tailor bird."

"You are very kind, Uncle Wiggily," spoke Lulu, "but if I go there I may not get back in time for the party, and I want to wear my new hat to it, very much."

"Ha! I see!" cried the bunny uncle. "You want to look nice at the party. Well, that's right, of course. And I don't believe the tailor bird could clean your new hat in time, for it is so fancy she would have to be very careful of it.

"But you can do as I did, make a hat of ferns, and wear that to Nannie Wagtail's party. I'll help you."

"Oh, how kind you are!" cried the little duck girl.

So she went along with Uncle Wiggily to where the ferns grew in the wood, leaving her regular hat at the tailor bird's nest to be cleaned and pressed.

Uncle Wiggily made Lulu the cutest hat out of fern leaves. Oh, I wish you could have seen it. There wasn't one like it not even in the five and ten cent store.

"Wear that to Nannie's party, Lulu," said the rabbit gentleman, and Lulu did, the hat being fastened to her feathers with a long pin made from the stem of a fern. And when Lulu arrived at the party all the animal girls cried out:

"Oh, what a sweet, lovely, cute, dear, cunning, swell and stylish hat! Where did you get it?"

"Uncle Wiggily made it," answered Lulu, and all the girls said they were going to get one just like it. And they did, so that fern hats became very fashionable and stylish in Woodland, and Lulu had a fine time at the party.

So this teaches us that even a mud puddle is of some use, and if the rubber plant doesn't stretch too far, and tickle the gold fish under the chin to make it sneeze, the next story will be about Uncle Wiggily and the currants.

STORY VIII

UNCLE WIGGILY AND THE CURRANTS

"Where are you going today, Uncle Wiggily?" asked Nurse Jane Fuzzy Wuzzy, the muskrat lady housekeeper, as she saw the farmer rabbit gentleman start out of his hollow stump house one morning.

"Over to my currant bushes," he answered. "You know I grow nice, red currants on my farm, as well as carrots and cabbage. I want to see if the currants are ripe enough to pick."

"And if they are," went on Nurse Jane, "I think it would be a good thing for you to bring some home so I could make jam."

"Fine!" cried the bunny uncle, jumping up and down on the end of his little tail. Then he was so glad that he sang this funny song:

"Jam, jam! Red currant jam!
You ask if I'm happy,
I'll say that I am.
No matter what happens, I'm jolly you see,
For Miss Fuzzy Wuzzy's so pleasant to me!"

Then Uncle Wiggily started across his farm to

the place where the currant bushes grew, with
their clusters of red fruit, hanging dingling, dan-
gling down—O! like the tails of Bo Peep's lost
sheep.

"Yes, there are plenty of currants for jam, and
also enough for a pie, I think," said Uncle Wiggily, as he kindly told some worms to stop eating
the green leaves of the bushes, for the worms were
making sandwiches of them.

The bunny uncle was sort of patting himself on
his whiskers, to think what a nice farm he had,
when all of a sudden he heard a little voice asking:

"Oh, may I have some?"

"Ha! I wonder who that is?" asked Uncle
Wiggily, turning quickly, and hoping it would
not happen to be the fuzzy fox or the skillery-
scalery alligator with tortoise-shell goggles on.
But it was only Susie Littletail, the rabbit girl.

"Ha! What do you want, Susie?" asked Uncle
Wiggily, kindly and politely.

"Some of those nice, red beads," spoke Susie,
pointing to the bushes. "I want them to make a
necklace on a string."

"Ha! Those are not red beads," said the bunny
uncle with a laugh. "They are red currants. I
will give you as many as you want, Susie, but

don't try to eat them unless you sprinkle lots of sugar on them."

"Why not?" Susie wanted to know.

"Because they are specially and double extra strong and sour," answered the bunny uncle. "String them on a long thread of grass for a coral necklace, if you like, Susie, but don't eat the red currant beads, unless you want your mouth to get all puckered up."

"I won't," promised Susie.

Then Uncle Wiggily gave her some of the red currants, and she strung them on a long, thin thread of grass to make a necklace, just as you make a daisy chain. Susie tasted one of the littlest red currants, and she puckered up her mouth after it, for the red fruit was very, very sour.

"Well, Uncle Wiggily," said the little rabbit girl at last, "my necklace is made now, and I guess I'll run and play with Squeaky Eeky, the little cousin mouse. Here, I'll give you some of my sweet lollypop to take the sour taste out of your mouth if you happen to eat some sour currants by mistake."

"Oh, thank you," said Uncle Wiggily, politely, and then with a piece of Susie's red colored lollypop in his paw, he went on looking at his currant bushes, while Susie hopped off down the road.

Not long after this Uncle Wiggily heard a harsh voice behind him saying:

"Well, whenever you are finished, you may come with me!"

"Come with you!" cried the rabbit gentleman, surprised like." Come with you?

"Yes, I've caught you again!" and there stood the bad old fox, all ready to grab our Uncle Wiggily. There was no way for the rabbit gentleman to get away, or escape, for the currant bushes were on all sides of him except one, and in that place stood the fox.

"Oh, dear!" sadly said the bunny chap. "What shall I do?"

"Come with me, of course," answered the fox, grinning and showing his teeth. "We shall dine together."

Uncle Wiggily knew what this meant—that the fox would do all the eating. So the bunny gentleman tried to think of a way out. Then he looked at the piece of red lollypop Susie had given him, and next he looked at the red currants, growing on bushes all around him. Then he said to the fox:

"Before you dine, would you not like to taste something good?"

"If you mean that lollypop—yes," answered the fox. "Hand it over!"

But instead of giving him the lollypop Uncle Wiggily behind his back slyly picked a bunch of the sour, red currants and gave them to the fox. The bad creature, thinking it was a lollypop, chewed them at once. Then a funny look came over his face. His mouth all puckered up as small as a thimble, and making a most distressful and apolegetic face he cried:

"Oh, wow! Oh, vinegar and lemons! My mouth is so puckered that I can't open it to eat you. Oh, what a trick you played on me! Oh wow!"

And then, lashing himself with his tail, away ran the fox to get some sugar to take the sour, puckery red currant taste out of his mouth, and Uncle Wiggily wasn't hurt after all, you see.

But if the haystack doesn't fall down at the barn dance and get all covered with strawberries, so it looks like a long cake, I'll tell you next about Uncle Wiggily and the green apples.

STORY IX

UNCLE WIGGILY AND THE GREEN APPLES

"What's the matter now, Uncle Wiggily?" asked Nurse Jane Fuzzy Wuzzy, the muskrat lady housekeeper one morning, as she saw the bunny gentleman standing on the front porch of his hollow stump farmhouse, looking as though he did not know what to do. "Are you in trouble? Have the carrots on your farm tickled the string beans, or did the onion make tears come in the eyes of the potatoes?"

"Neither one," answered Uncle Wiggily. "It's all on account of the animal boys and the green apples on my farm."

"Green apples!" exclaimed Nurse Jane. "Animal boys?"

"Yes," answered Uncle Wiggily. "Sammie Littletail, the rabbit chap; Johnnie and Billie Bushytail, the squirrels; Jackie and Peetie Bow Wow, the puppy dogs, and lots of their chums, are taking green apples from my farm, and eating them."

"You don't mind that, do you?" asked Nurse Jane.

"I don't mind the apples," said Uncle Wiggily,

52

"but I don't want those animal chaps to be made
ill eating them. I guess I'll just take a hop, skip
and a jump over to that part of my farm where
the green apples grow, and see what I can do to
stop those little chaps from getting them."

"Better take your umbrella," said Nurse Jane.
"It looks like rain."

"I will take it," said the bunny gentleman, and
holding the rain-shedder in his paw he started
over toward the green-apple-tree-part of his farm.

It was a nice, warm, pleasant summer day, and
when he had hopped over a few fences, crawled
under some stone walls and skipped through the
green woods, the bunny gentleman found himself at his orchard of apple trees.

"Well, none of the animal chaps are here now,"
he said to himself, looking around. "But they
will soon be. I'll just wait until they come, and
then I'll tell them they must take no more of the
green apples."

So down sat the bunny uncle under the tree to
wait.

As I have said, it was a warm, pleasant day,
so it is not surprising that Uncle Wiggily fell
asleep on the bed of soft, green moss that grew
around the tree.

How long he slumbered he did not know, but
he was awakened, all of a sudden, by feeling some-

thing like a rough nutmeg grater, or a file, or cocoanut scraper being drawn over his pink, twinkling nose.

"My goodness me, sakes alive, What's the matter?" cried Uncle Wiggily, sneezing and jumping up.

Then he saw the bad old skillery-scalery alligator, with the humps on his tail, standing near, and slowly opening and closing his mouth.

"Oh, my!" said Uncle Wiggily, surprised like. "Did you wake me up?"

"I guess I did," spoke the 'gator. "I just brushed you with my nutmeg grater tail. I wanted to wake you up because you and I are going on a little picnic together. I am going to have the best time at the picnic. You are to be the lunch basket, so to speak."

"Oh, dear!" cried Uncle Wiggily again. "I don't want to go to lunch with you," and he well knew that he very likely would be eaten by the skillery-scalery creature.

"No matter what you want—come along with me!" cried the 'gator, most savage like and impolitely. "If you do not come by yourself I will carry you, for I am very strong."

"Are you, really?" asked Uncle Wiggily, as if he didn't know.

"Of course I am!" cried the 'gator, a bit proud like.

Then, all of a sudden, Uncle Wiggily thought of something. He looked up at the tree on which were many hard, round, green apples—as hard as stones, almost. Indeed it is a wonder how boys ever bite them. Next the rabbit gentleman looked at the alligator who was waiting to carry him away.

"Do you think you are strong enough to shake and jiggle this tree?" asked Mr. Longears.

"Of course, I am," answered the 'gator. "But why do you want it jiggled?"

"Well, let me see if you can do it," went on the bunny chap. "I'd like to see you shake the tree before you take me away."

"That is very easy for me to do," went on the proud alligator. "With one blow of my strong tail I can jiggle this tree like anything. After I do that I will take you away with me."

Uncle Wiggily raised his umbrella. The alligator shook his tail, hit the tree with it as hard as he could bang, and then:

"Bango! Cracko! Smasho!"

Down fell a shower of the hard, green apples, like stones. They hit the alligator on his nose and his toes, and he was so pelted and sore that he cried:

"Oh, wow! This is no place for me! It is raining hard, green bullets!" And then he ran away and didn't bother Uncle Wiggily at all. And the bunny gentleman, even though he was under the apple tree, did not get hit because he had raised his umbrella over his head.

And all the green apples were shaken off the tree so the animal boys could not eat any more of them and be made ill. Thus, everything came out all right, you see, and if the string bean doesn't wind itself around the cucumber and tie the sweet potato in a hard knot I'll tell you next about Uncle Wiggily and the peaches.

STORY X

"Where are you going, Uncle Wiggily?" asked Sammie Littletail, the rabbit boy, one day, as he saw the bunny man come down out of his hollow stump farm house and start to hop across the fields and green meadows.

"Why, I am going for a walk to see how the fruit and vegetables are growing on my farm," Uncle Wiggily answered. "Do you want to come with me?"

"There are no more green apples, are there?" Sammie wanted to know, making his pink nose, which was just like Uncle Wiggily's, twinkle in the sun.

"No more, I am glad to say," answered the rabbit. "The skillery scalery alligator knocked all the green apples off, so you boys could not eat them, and make yourselves ill. All that are left are ripe ones, but they will not be ready to eat for some time."

"Oh, dear!" said Sammie, sort of sighing like.

"What's the matter?" Uncle Wiggily wanted to know.

"I'm so hungry," went on the little rabbit chap.

57

"I was counting on eating apples, but if there aren't any—"

"What would you say to peaches?" asked the bunny man.

"Peaches? Oh, my!" cried Sammie, smacking his lips and clapping his paws. "That's just fine! But where are some?"

"I have a peach tree on my farm," went on Uncle Wiggily. "The peaches ought to be ripe now. We'll take a walk over and see."

Through the woods and over the fields went the bunny uncle and the rabbit chap. It did not take them long to reach the place where the peach tree grew, and from the limbs were hanging many beautiful red-cheeked peaches, all ready to be eaten.

"Oh, yum-yum!" cried Sammie, happy-like.

"I think I'll eat a few myself," said the bunny gentleman.

So, first spreading a soft carpet of bunches of green grass under the tree, Uncle Wiggily and Sammie knocked down some of the fruit. It fell, bounced up in the air, they caught it and made a little peach pile at the foot of the tree.

"We have enough," said the rabbit gentleman at length. "Let's sit down and eat some, Sammie. And I will take home a few in the top of my tall silk hat so Nurse Jane can make a peach shortcake."

The bunny gentleman and the little rabbit boy were eating the soft, tender and sweet peaches, talking about how good they were, and how nice it was to have a farm where you could grow all the things you needed for your meals, when, all of a sudden, down at the end of the peach orchard there was a rustling in the bushes, and Sammie cried:

"Look there, Uncle Wiggily!"

Uncle Wiggily looked. He saw a bad old nose-pinching kangaroo animal with such long hind legs that it can almost jump up to the moon.

"Are you Uncle Wiggily?" asked the kangaroo, growling like.

"I am," was the answer.

"Then you're the one I'm looking for," went on the nose-pinching chap. "The ear-scratching cat and the tail-pulling chimpanzee told me about you. I haven't practiced pinching any noses for a long while. Just come here until I pinch yours a bit."

"Oh, I don't want to," spoke Uncle Wiggily, sort of shy-like and bashful.

"You must!" cried the nose-pinching kangaroo. "If you don't I'll take you away with me and—"

"Throw peaches at him, Uncle Wiggily!" suddenly whispered Sammie. "Throw the peaches
at him! We have more than we can eat."

"That's the idea! The very thing!" Uncle
Wiggily said. "You throw some and I'll throw
some more at the bad chap!"

Together they threw a lot of peaches.

"Squash! Squash! Squish!" smashed the red-
cheeked peaches on the end of the nose of the bad
kangaroo.

"Pooh! Nonsense! Do you think I mind such
soft things as peaches?" he cried. "I'll carry you
away for all of them, and pinch your nose, too!"

Straight at Uncle Wiggily he ran, and then
when the bunny gentleman did not know what to
do, Sammie suddenly cried:

"Oh, Uncle Wiggily, there are hard stones inside the peaches. If we take them out and throw
them at this nose-pinching kangeroo chap, we
may yet drive him away."

"Very good! Do it quickly!" cried Mr. Longears. "Hurry, Sammie!"

Then Uncle Wiggily and the bunny boy broke
open the soft peaches, which the kangaroo did
not mind any more than so many pieces of chocolate cake, and the two bunnies took out from inside the peaches the hard stones. These they
threw at the unpleasant animal, and then that

bad old nose-pinching chap, feeling the stones strike him, cried:

"Oh, dear! Oh, woe is me! Oh, jitney buses and hard-headed lead pencils! I guess I made a mistake. I don't mind soft peaches, but I don't like hard stones! I don't want to pinch any noses today!"

Then he ran away, not bothering Uncle Wiggily or Sammie any more. So this teaches us it it is a good thing that all peaches have stones.

And if the umbrella doesn't pull the mosquito screens out of the windows, to play tag with on the front porch with the roller skates, I'll tell you next of Uncle Wiggily and the rubber plant.

STORY XI

UNCLE WIGGILY AND THE RUBBER PLANT

"Here is something for your farm, Uncle Wiggily," said Nurse Jane Fuzzy Wuzzy, the muskrat lady housekeeper, as she came out one morning, on the front porch of the hollow stump house, where the rabbit gentleman was looking up at the sky to see if it might shed tears of rain.

"Something for my farm? That is very nice," Uncle Wiggily answered with a smile that made his whiskers look as curly as a carpenter's shaving. "What is it?"

"A rubber plant," answered Nurse Jane.

"A rubber plant!" cried Uncle Wiggily. "How nice ! I suppose it has rubber balls growing on it instead of peaches or pears."

"No," spoke Nurse Jane. "It hasn't."

"Then does it grow stretcher rubber bands, that play nice jolly music-marching tunes?" asked the bunny gentleman. "Come to think of it, I'd rather have a rubber plant that grew rubber bands than anything else. I am so fond of music!"

"I am sorry to disappoint you," said the muskrat lady, "but, as a matter of fact," and she spoke just like a school teacher on her vacation, "as a matter of fact the rubber plant I am going to give you for your farm doesn't grow rubber bands."

"Then what does grow on it, or come off it?" the bunny uncle wanted to know.

"Just rubber leaves," answered Nurse Jane. "Nice big, glossy, green leaves grow on the rubber plant, and make it pretty to look at. That is all. It is good to see."

Uncle Wiggily scratched his chin with his left hind foot, and looked as though he was thinking very hard.

"To tell you the truth, Nurse Jane," he said, "I haven't much room on my farm for anything that just looks nice. I must raise things that are good to eat—such as corn and peas and beans, or potatoes, or carrots."

"I see," spoke Nurse Jane, sort of sad like. "Then you don't want my nice, pretty rubber plant, that I bought at the five and six cent store?"

"Oh, of course I want it!" cried Mr. Longears, seeing that Nurse Jane would feel badly if he did not take her present. "Only if it doesn't grow rubber balls or gum drops or—Oh, well, never mind. I guess it's time I had something on my farm that is nice to look at, even if you can't eat it," he went on. "Thank you very much, Nurse Jane. I'll set out your rubber plant over in the meadow, where the cows can see it. They like green things."

So Uncle Wiggily set out the rubber plant and then, as he was very busy about his farm, hoeing the corn, pulling the weeds out of the onion bed and sprinkling Paris green on the potatoes, for a time he forgot all about Nurse Jane's present.

But the rubber plant did not forget about itself. It grew and grew and grew, until it was large and strong, with big, stretchy, glossy green leaves on it.

One day Uncle Wiggily was riding around his farm in his automobile, watching things grow. He saw the cabbages getting nice big heads on them, the peas and beans were filling out, and the eyes of the potatoes were blinking at the ears of corn, to see which would be ripe first. And the corn-ears were listening to the dew drop.

"Everything seems to be coming along all right," said Uncle Wiggily, as he started his auto again. "I guess I'll go back to my hollow stump farm house and have supper." So back he started, but he had not gone far before all of a sudden he heard a sound like: "Hiss-s-s-s!"

"Oh, dear," cried the bunny uncle. "One of my auto tires has a hole in it, and the air is sissing out!"

And, surely enough, that was what happened. A sharp stone had made a hole in the bologna sausage tire on one of the wheels of the rabbit gentleman's auto, and he had to stop.

"Well, well!" he cried, as he got out to look at it. "This is too bad! I can't run my automobile with a hole in the tire, and yet I must get home before——"

And just then there was a rustling in the bushes, and out jumped a bad old fox.

"Ah, ha! This time I have you!" he cried to the bunny gentleman. "You can't get away from me now with your burst tire. Your auto won't go! I have you!"

"So you have!" sadly said Uncle Wiggily. And the fox was just going to grab him when another voice suddenly spoke and said:

"Quick, Uncle Wiggily! Take some of my leaves and some sticky gum from the pine tree near you, and mend the hole in your tire. Then it will hold the air and you can ride home and get away from the fox. Quick! Paste one of my leaves over the hole in the tire!"

"Who are you?" asked Uncle Wiggily.

"Nurse Jane's rubber plant," was the answer.

Then the bunny gentleman took some of the stretchy, rubbery leaves and plastered them over the hole in the auto tire with some pine tree sticky gum. Next he blew some air in the mended tire, and, before the fox could grab him, away went Mr. Longears in his auto as nicely as you please, and the fox couldn't run fast enough to catch him.

"I'm sorry I thought your rubber plant was of little use," said Uncle Wiggily to Nurse Jane that night when he was safely home. "It saved my life. Now I know that things can be beautiful to look at and useful at the same time."

And I guess you children know that too. So, if the chocolate cake doesn't turn into a pumpkin pie and hide in the sugar bowl, where the cream puff can't find it to play marbles, I'll tell you next about Uncle Wiggily and the corncobs.

STORY XII

UNCLE WIGGILY AND THE CORNCOBS

"Where are you going today?" asked Nurse Jane Fuzzy Wuzzy, the muskrat lady, as she saw Uncle Wiggily Longears, the rabbit gentleman, starting out of his hollow stump farm house one morning. "Are you going to pick beans, or smell the perfume of the cauliflower?"

"Neither one, if you please," answered the rabbit gentleman, with a polite bow, as he twinkled his pink nose like a leaf of lettuce with a dew drop in the center. "I am going over to the far, green field, where my corn is growing, and husk it. Then I am going to rub from the corncob the yellow kernels, so they can be ground up into yellow meal, to make Johnnie cakes."

"And won't there be any Sammie or Billie or Susie or Lulu cakes?" asked Nurse Jane, smiling.

"Oh, yes, of course, there will be," answered the bunny gentleman. "Johnnie cake is only a name. Any of the animal children may have some of the cake made from corn if you bake one."

"Then I'll certainly bake enough for all," said the muskrat lady, laughing.

So Uncle Wiggily started across his farm to

where the corn was growing. It was a new kind,
and became ripe very early.

Sitting down in the middle of the field, in the
shade of a pile of cornstalks, which he cut down
with his knife, Uncle Wiggily began to shell off
the yellow kernels. The kernels he put in a pan
that Nurse Jane had given him, letting them fall
into it with a rattle-te-bang like the sound of rain
on the shingle roof at night.

The corncobs, which he did not want, the rabbit gentleman tossed to one side. He was working away, shelling the corn, tossing the cobs over
his ears, and wondering what he would have for
dinner, when, all of a sudden, he heard a little
voice asking:

"Uncle Wiggily, may I have these old cobs?"

"Why, of course, you may," answered the
bunny gentleman. And then he thought he had
better look and see who was speaking, as, for
all he knew, it might be the bad old skillery-scalery alligator, or the fuzzy fox.

But it was not—it was only Jackie Bow-Wow,
the little puppy dog chap.

"What do you want of the corncobs, Jackie?"
asked Uncle Wiggily, curious like.

"Oh, I'm going to make something of them,"
said the little puppy chap. "May I have a lot of
them?"

"As many as you like," answered the bunny man. "I shall be glad to get rid of them, as they are of no use to me. All corncobs are good for, as far as I know, are to make pipes, and, as I don't smoke on account of my rheumatism, I don't need a pipe. I don't want the corncobs—they are no good. Take them all."

But you just wait and see how good the corncobs were going to be to Uncle Wiggily.

The old rabbit gentleman kept on shelling corn, and tossing the empty cobs in a pile behind him. From there Jackie Bow Wow picked them up, and Uncle Wiggily did not notice what the puppy dog chap did with them.

A little later along came Grandfather Goosey Gander, the goose gentleman, waddling through the cornfield just like an elephant picking up peanuts.

"Well, well! Uncle Wiggily!" Grandpa Goosey exclaimed. "I certainly am glad to see you! I haven't had a game of Scotch checkers with you in a long while. Can't we play now?"

"We have no checkers or a checker board," answered the bunny uncle.

"We can easily mark out the squares of a checker board on the ground," said Grandpa Goosey, "and for checkers we can take kernels of corn. You take the red ones, and I'll take yellow."

So the two friends began to play Scotch checkers. That is a game in which you either have to make a hop-Scotch or eat butterscotch, or something Scotch, as you play.

All of a sudden, just as Uncle Wiggily was jumping one of his red checker-kings over two of Grandpa Goosey's yellow corn checker-men, there was a growling sound at the end of the cornfield and out popped a big, bad fox.

"Ah, ha!" barked the fox, just like a dog. "I am in luck today. I will have two good meals—a rabbit and a goose. Ha! Ha!"

"Oh, dear!" sadly said Uncle Wiggily. "It's too bad!"

"It certainly is!" cried Grandpa Goosey Gander. "You are one and I am one, and one and one make two bad! But it's the fox who really is bad. He is one very bad. Do you think he will eat us?"

"That's just what I am going to do!" cried the fox. "Here I come!" and with that he made a jump for the two friends, but just then a sly little voice said:

"Uncle Wiggily! Grandpa Goosey! Come in here, quick!"

"In where?" asked the bunny uncle, looking all around.

"In the strong house that I made of the empty corncobs," was the answer. "Come in and hide and the fox can't get you," and there stood Jackie Bow Wow, the puppy boy, at the door of a house he had made of the corncobs.

It was a large enough house to hold him and Uncle Wiggily and Grandpa Goosey. Into it they jumped, and Jackie quickly closed the door tightly. Up rushed the fox, but he could not get in the strong corncob house and the rabbit, the goose and the puppy dog boy were safe.

Then the fox, clinking his teeth, because he was so disappointed, ran away, and he had to go to a restaurant for his dinner.

"Ha, I guess corncobs are of some use after all," said Uncle Wiggily. And if the soap bubble doesn't go up like a balloon and take the wash boiler with it, I'll tell you about Uncle Wiggily and the well.

STORY XIII

UNCLE WIGGILY AND THE WELL

"My, my This is too bad! Quite too bad!" exclaimed Uncle Wiggily Longears, the rabbit gentleman, as he hopped out of his hollow stump farmhouse one day and looked up at the sky. "This is dreadful."

"What is?" asked Nurse Jane Fuzzy Wuzzy, the muskrat lady housekeeper, making her tail curl. "Are you afraid it is going to rain?"

"No, I'm afraid it isn't," Uncle Wiggily said.

"Well, that's funny," went on Nurse Jane. "As a rule you don't like rain, because it makes your rheumatism worse."

"Oh, I'd even be willing to suffer some pains of rheumatism for the sake of rain now," went on the bunny uncle. "You see it has not rained in a long while, and my farm is so dry that it is all cracking open. The corn, peas, beans and carrots will not grow if they do not soon get watered. That is why I am looking at the sky, to see if it will not rain," and the rabbit gentleman looked first with one eye and then with the other up at the sky, but not a drop of water could he see.

For two days more it did not rain, and then, finally, Uncle Wiggily said to Nurse Jane:

"Well, there is only one thing for me to do, and that is to go over and dip some water up out of the well on the far end of my farm and dampen the things myself with the sprinkling can."

"Oh, will you have to do that?" Nurse Jane wanted to know."

"I fear I shall have to," the bunny uncle said.

"Well, don't get your feet wet," went on Nurse Jane. "If you do, you may catch the ker-snuffles and the akerchoos-zium."

"I wouldn't want that to happen," Uncle Wiggily said, with a laugh, "so I'll put on my rubber boots and my rain coat when I water my farm from the well."

That afternoon he started for the far end of his farm, where it was very extra dry. At that place was an old well, with a bucket on the end of a chain.

You could let the bucket down into the well, where it would fill itself with water, and then you could pull it up.

Uncle Wiggily did this, pouring the water into his sprinkling can and splashing it over the hot, dusty and thirsty vegetables of his farm.

And, as soon as the water drops fell on them, or

on the dry ground in which they grew, the plants raised their leaves and whispered:

"Oh, how lovely that is! How nice it makes us feel."

"I am glad you like it," said Uncle Wiggily, and he kept on drawing more water.

He had almost finished sprinkling the plants, and was thinking about going back to his hollow stump house to get something to eat, which Nurse Jane would have ready for him, when, as he was pulling up the last bucket of water, something away down in the bottom of the well caught the edge of the pail-bucket and Uncle Wiggily could not pull it up.

"Ha! This is queer! The pail is caught fast in the well," said the bunny gentleman. "I must pull hard to get it out and finish my watering."

So he pulled and pulled and pulled again on the rope that was tied to the bucket, but the more he pulled the tighter the bucket seemed held fast.

"Well, I must get it up," said Uncle Wiggily to himself, twinkling his pink nose, bracing his feet against the edge of the well, and folding back his ears so they would not get in his way. "I need this water. I guess the pail must be caught on the edge of a stone."

Uncle Wiggily was pulling as hard as he could,

when, all of a sudden, he heard a voice behind him
saying:

"What are you trying to do, pull up the bottom of the well?"

"Oh, no, indeed," answered the rabbit man,
and, turning around, there stood the bad old skillery-scalery alligator, smiling so wide and broadly
that you would have thought the top of his head
might fly off. "I'm just trying to pull up the
bucket of water," went on Uncle Wiggily.

"You needn't bother any more about it," said
the alligator. "Leave it there. I'm going to take
you away with me."

"Oh, please don't!" begged Uncle Wiggily,
sad-like.

"Yes, I shall," answered the impolite alligator.
"Come along!"

"Oh, before I go," cried Uncle Wiggily, "will
you not kindly pull up this bucket of water for
me. I need it to water my farm vegetables. I can
not pull it up, but you can, as you are so strong."

"Yes, I am very strong," said the 'gator, sort
of proud like and supercilious. "I'll pull up the
bucket for you, and then I'll take you off to my
den."

The skillery-scalery alligator took hold of the
rope. He pulled once, he pulled twice and he
pulled three times, and then—presto-changeo!

All of a sudden he pulled so hard that he broke the rope, and head over heels he went in a back somersault, and he kept on tumbling and rolling over backward until he rolled down hill, and before he could roll back again Uncle Wiggily hopped safely away to his hollow stump farm house. And then it rained and Uncle Wiggily didn't have to water his farm.

So the alligator, with the bumps on his tail, didn't get the bunny gentleman after all, you see, just for showing off how strong he was, and in the next story, if the sweet potato doesn't try to swim in the bean soup and throw oranges at the chocolate cake, I'll tell you next about Uncle Wiggily and the pie-plant.

STORY XIV

UNCLE WIGGILY AND THE PIE PLANT

"Oh, I feel so happy; I feel so very fine; 'cause the nicest days of all the year are those of summertime!"

That's what Uncle Wiggily Longears, the nice old rabbit gentleman, sang as he hopped down off the porch of his hollow stump farm house one morning and started across the fields with his hoe over his shoulder.

"My! But you are jolly today!" exclaimed Nurse Jane Fuzzy Wuzzy, the muskrat lady housekeeper, as she finished washing the breakfast dishes.

"I am jolly," answered Uncle Wiggily. "Everything on my farm is growing so nicely since it rained after I tried to water the vegetables from the well, where the old skillery-scalery alligator bumped his nose the other day. Everything is fine, and today I am going over in my field and dig some sweet potatoes."

"And I'll make you a sweet-potato pie!" said Nurse Jane, with a smile.

"That will be lovely!" cried the bunny uncle, and he blew a kiss from the tip of his paw to the muskrat lady, for he was very polite, even if he was a rabbit.

Well, pretty soon, in a little while, not so very long, Uncle Wiggily came to the place where the sweet potatoes grew under the ground. He took off his coat, pulled his straw hat down over his ears so he would not get sun burned, and began digging.

Out rolled the brown sweet potatoes from the hills of dirt where they had been growing. Uncle Wiggily picked them up and put them in his basket. He was thinking how good the pie would taste when Nurse Jane had baked it, when, all of a sudden, he was surprised to hear behind him a voice saying:

"Well, you may stop work, now!"

"My goodness me, sakes alive, and some huckleberry pudding!" cried the bunny uncle. "Who is there?"

"I am," said the voice of the fuzzy fox, and there, surely enough he was, sitting down and looking at Mr. Longears.

"What do you want?" Uncle Wiggily begged to know.

"You!" snarled the fox. "Stop your work and come with me. I surely have you this time. You shan't get away!"

Uncle Wiggily didn't know what to do. He

didn't want to go away with the fox, and I guess you wouldn't either; would you?

No, I thought not. Well, the old rabbit gentleman looked around, hoping he could find some way to run off and be safe when, all at once, the fox pointed to some big, broad, green leaves, growing near where Uncle Wiggily was digging the sweet potatoes, and the fox asked:

"What are they?"

"That is a pie plant," answered Uncle Wiggily, politely, for he was polite, even to a fox.

"A pie plant, eh?" went on the fuzzy creature. "Well, if that is a pie-plant, just pick for me a cherry pie and I'll eat it before I take you away with me. Pick me a pie!"

"But I can't," said Uncle Wiggily, flustered like.

"I thought you said that was a pie plant," went on the fox.

"So it is," said Uncle Wiggily. "But you don't understand. First you have to pull up the stalks of the plant and cook them into rhubarb. Then you make a pie and——"

"Nonsense!" cried the fox. "If that is a pie plant it must have pies growing on it. Now you must either pick me a pie, that I can eat right now, without waiting to have it cooked, or I'll do something to you!"

Poor Uncle Wiggily didn't know what to say. Well he knew that no ready-baked pie grew on the pie-plant, and especially no cherry ones. What was he to do? All of a sudden he heard, from under one of the leaves of the plant, a little voice whispering:

"Uncle Wiggily! Ask the bad fox if he'll let you go if you give him a pie."

"Eh, what's that? Who are you?" asked the rabbit gentleman.

"Never mind, you ask him," went on the voice. "Ask him if he wants a pie."

So Uncle Wiggily said:

"If I give you a pie from this plant, Mr. Fox, will you let me go?"

"Maybe," answered the fuzzy creature, shy like and non-committal. "Anyway, I'll bite you if I don't get a pie."

The bunny uncle turned to the big green leaf again. Out from under it slid a big pie. Not stopping to ask how it got there. Uncle Wiggily quickly passed it over to the fox, saying:

"There you are!"

The fox bit the pie, but suddenly his face all became wrinkled up and he cried: "Oh, ouch! Oh, Wow! Oh, my mouth is all puckered! I can't bite even a lemon! Oh, woe is me!" and away he ran to the drug store to get something

with which to unpucker his mouth, leaving Uncle
Wiggily safe, and not hurt a bit.

"Where did that pie come from?" asked the
bunny uncle. "I'm sure it never grew on the
plant."

"It didn't," answered the little voice. "I had
it with me. It was a cherry pie I got at the store
for my mother, but I guess the baker forgot to
put any sugar in it. That's what made it so sour
for the fox," and out came Sammy Littletail, the
rabbit boy.

"Well, it's a good thing for me that it was
sour," said Uncle Wiggily with a smile as the little rabbit chap hopped out from under the plant.

Sammie was on his way home from the bakery
when he happened to see the fox trying to catch
the bunny man, but Sammie saved him by hiding
under the big leaves and by handing out the pie
just in time.

And if the mooley cow doesn't step on the rubber ball, and knock all the wind out, so it can't
catch its breath, when it plays tag with the goat's
express wagon, I'll tell you next about Uncle
Wiggily and the bird seed.

UNCLE WIGGILY AND THE BIRD SEED

"Uncle Wiggily," spoke Lulu Wibblewobble, the little girl duck, one morning, as she toddled over to the hollow stump house of the old rabbit gentleman, "is there any part of your farm you are not using?"

"Not using?" asked Mr. Longears. "What do you mean, Lulu? I use nearly all of my farm to grow fruits and vegetables. If you want anything like that——"

"No, I just want a little patch of land where I can plant something myself," said the duck girl.

"Oh, I see!" cried Uncle Wiggily, making his pink nose twinkle like a piece of frosted cake. "You want to make a little garden."

"That's it," said Lulu, quacking her yellow bill. "I only want a little piece of land, where I can plant some seeds."

"You shall have it," spoke Uncle Wiggily. "Let me see now. I think I'll give you a seed place over where I used to grow some lettuce. The green leaves are all done growing now, and

82

the little garden is vacant. You may have it. But what are you going to plant?"

Lulu took some seeds out from under her wing. They were of three or four different kinds, some large and some small.

"My! Those are funny seeds!" Uncle Wiggily said, laughing. "What do you expect to grow from them Lulu?"

"Canary birds," answered the little duck girl.

"Canary birds!" cried the rabbit gentleman. "What put that notion in your head?"

"Why, in a drug store window I saw a sign which said canary bird seed was only ten cents a package. So I went in and bought some. I thought it would be nicer to raise my own canary birds than to buy them in the little wooden cages at the fine and ten cent store," Lulu said. "And, when the little birds pop out of the ground, I'll let them all go, for I don't like to see them in cages. I wouldn't like to be in a cage myself; would you, Uncle Wiggily?"

"No, indeed. But listen, Lulu, as the telephone girl says, this is only seed for canary birds to eat. You can no more plant it, and have canary birds grow us from it, than could Jackie and Peetie Bow Wow plant bones and expect to have ham sandwiches spring up, or have umbrellas grow on rubber plants. It can't be done."

Lulu looked sad for a little while. Then she said:

"Well, anyhow, Uncle Wiggily, even if I can't grow canary birds from seed, maybe I can raise something on your farm. May I have a little patch of your ground?"

"You certainly may, all for yourself," said the bunny uncle kindly, "but don't expect to raise any sweet singing canary birds from seeds, Lulu."

"I won't," promised Lulu. Then with Charlie, the chicken chap, to help her scratch up the ground, Lulu planted the seeds. Each day after that she brought water and sprinkled it all around to make the ground moist so the seeds could more easily push themselves up through it. And each day Lulu went to the little garden patch which Uncle Wiggily had set aside for her on his farm, and she hoped even though Uncle Wiggily said it could not happen, that some canary birds might appear.

After a while the seeds sprouted and grew. Tiny green leaves came up, growing larger and larger each day as the sun smiled on them, until they turned into quite large bushes. Then one day Lulu the duck, who had waddled over to her garden to see what was going on, noticed some yellow things fluttering among the green branches that had grown from her seed.

"Oh, they're birds! I believe they're birds!" she cried, clapping her wings. "Uncle Wiggily made a mistake. Canary birds came from my seeds, after all!"

And, surely enough, there were canary birds perched in among the green bushes, chirping and singing most sweetly.

"I'm going to tell Uncle Wiggily," said Lulu. "He will surely be surprised!"

Taking one more look at the yellow birds in the green bushes, away flapped the duck girl to the hollow stump farm house.

"Oh, Uncle Wiggily!" she cried. "Come with me, quick! The canary birds are there!"

"Where?" asked the bunny gentleman.

"In the seed bushes I planted. You said no birds would grow, but they did. The canary birds came!" And Lulu flapped her wings, and almost crowed, she was so excited.

"Well, this is very strange," said the bunny uncle. "I don't see how canary birds can grow from seed, and yet—well, I will go with you and look, Lulu."

And when Uncle Wiggily came to the field and saw the yellow birds fluttering in among the green bushes that had grown up from the seeds, he said, laughingly:

"I see how it is, Lulu. You planted canary bird seed. The seed grew and brought forth other seeds. Then the yellow canary birds, and the other birds, flying in the air, saw the growing seeds and came to eat them. That's what they are doing now in the bushes. From all over they have come here to eat your seeds."

"Oh, so they have!" cried Lulu. "Well, any-how, I'm glad they can eat the seeds when they are hungry!"

And the birds were glad, too, and sang most sweetly to thank Lulu for growing seeds for them to eat. And so, even if she did not make some canary birds grow, the little duck girl gave them a fine treat.

And, if the cornstarch pudding doesn't go out in the clothes basket where the salt spoon can't find it to sprinkle sugar on the short cake, I'll tell you next about Uncle Wiggily and the eggs.

STORY XVI

UNCLE WIGGILY AND THE EGGS

One day, after Uncle Wiggily Longears, the rabbit gentleman, had awakened from a little sleep he had taken under an apple tree, he stretched his whiskers, twinkled his pink nose and then, opening his ears as wide as they would go, he said:

"Well, I guess I'll take a walk over to the far end of my farm and see how everything is growing."

"Isn't it pretty late in the afternoon to go to look at your farm?" asked Nurse Jane Fuzzy Wuzzy, the muskrat lady housekeeper. "Supper is almost ready."

"I won't be long," Uncle Wiggily said, picking up his tall silk hat and his red, white and blue striped rheumatism crutch. "I haven't had an adventure today, and the afternoon is just as good a time in which to find one as is the morning. So here I go!"

"Well, good luck to you," Nurse Jane said, with a cheerful wave of her tail as she went in to set the table for supper. "Oh, by the way!" she called to Uncle Wiggily. "You might gather

the eggs on your way back. It will save me
making a trip."

"I'll do it," the bunny uncle promised. "I'll
bring all the eggs."

For, you know, on his farm, just as on all
farms, there were chickens to lay eggs, otherwise
it wouldn't have been a farm.

On and on hopped Uncle Wiggily, until he
came to the far end of his land, where some sweet
potatoes were growing. The rabbit gentleman
tasted one of them, and, as they were not quite
sweet enough to suit him, he sprinkled on them
some sugar he had brought in his pocket.

"For I like my sweet potatoes good and sweet,"
he said. Having done this, he looked all around
for an adventure—which means something happening to you—but he could not seem to find any.

"Never mind," said Uncle Wiggily to himself.
"I'll go on back and gather the eggs. I may find
one there."

The hens and chickens on Uncle Wiggily's
farm laid their eggs in nests in different places.
Some chickens liked to go in the hen house, others
on the hay in the barn, and some crawled under
the place where Uncle Wiggily kept his automobile. So the rabbit gentleman or Nurse Jane—
whoever gathered the eggs—had to look in many
places.

Taking the basket which was always used for the eggs, the bunny uncle started to hunt them. He found some in the hay, and some in the straw, and a few were in the grass back of where the tall hollyhock flowers grew.

"Well, I have quite a basketful of eggs," said the bunny gentleman to himself, when he had gathered nearly all on his farm. "But I know where there is one more nest."

However, when he reached it there were no eggs in it. The chickens had moved away. Oh, yes, there was just one egg, but it was not a real one. It was a hard stone, made white, and shaped like an egg, and it was a make-believe egg, such as are kept in most nests to make the chickens happy.

You know if a hen gets in a nest that already has an egg in it she thinks to herself:

"Pooh! What a mean, stingy little nest. Only one tiny egg! I wonder who could have laid it? I can do much better than that? Wait until they see my egg."

So she goes to work and lays a nice egg, and all the while the egg she saw in the nest is only a make-believe one, and not real at all.

It wouldn't do to keep a real, good egg in the nest all the while, for it might get broken. So

Uncle Wiggily used to put in pretend, stone or chalk ones.

"Well, since the chickens don't lay in this nest any more," said the bunny to himself, I'll just take this stone egg out and use it somewhere else."

He put the hard stone egg on top of his basket of good fresh eggs and started for his hollow stump farm house. He had not gone very far before, all of a sudden, out from behind a stone jumped the bad old ear-scratching cat.

"Yow! Yow!" howled the cat. "Once again I have caught you! And you have eggs, too, I see. Oh, I dearly love eggs! I'll have some of them first, before I scratch your ear."

Uncle Wiggily suddenly thought of a plan to fool that cat.

"Oh, you'll have some of these eggs; will you?" he cried. "Well, how will this one do for a starter? Do you like your eggs hard or soft?"

"Hard," answered the cat. "I like hard eggs."

"Then take this one," cried the bunny uncle, and with that he suddenly threw the hard, stone, make-believe egg at the bad ear-scratching cat.

Right on the cat's soft and tender nose the hard, make-believe egg landed, and the cat yowled:

"Oh, my! I didn't mean an egg as hard as

that! Oh, my poor nose! Oh, dear!" And then the cat ran away to get some court plaster to put on its nose; and so it didn't scratch Uncle Wiggily's ears or eat any eggs, either, and I think that served it right.

So here we are again at the end of the story, but if the June bug doesn't tickle the Katy-did and make her laugh right out loud in the moving picture show, I'll tell you next about Uncle Wiggily and the hollyhocks.

STORY XVII

UNCLE WIGGILY AND THE HOLLYHOCKS

"I hope you don't mind," said Nurse Jane Fuzzy Wuzzy, the muskrat lady housekeeper, one day, as she came up to where Uncle Wiggily Longears, the rabbit gentleman, was sitting on the front porch of his hollow stump farm house, with his tall silk hat full of ice water beside him, for it was very warm.

"Mind? Mind who—or what?" asked the bunny uncle, smiling so that his whiskers seemed to chase each other away around behind his ears. "I always mind what you say, and if you want me to go to the nine and ten cent store—"

"Oh, not at all, thank you!" exclaimed the muskrat lady. What I meant was, I hope you don't mind me asking them."

"Who?" went on Mr. Longears.

"Sammie and Susie Littletail, the rabbit children, Johnnie and Billie Bushytail, the squirrels, Jackie and Peetie Bow Wow, the puppy dogs, to say nothing of Bully and Bawly No-Tail, the frogs. I've asked them to come to a little garden party I'm giving this afternoon," said Nurse Jane. "I hope you don't mind."

"Not in the least!" cried Uncle Wiggily with a jolly laugh. "The more the merrier. But where are you giving the party?"

"In the garden in front of your farm," said Nurse Jane. "There are flowers in the garden—roses, lilies, phlox and hollyhocks. But the animal children will not hurt any of the blossoms."

"Bless their hearts, I know they won't!" exclaimed Uncle Wiggily, making his pink nose twinkle like a red necktie on the back of a trolley car. "Let them have all the fun they can."

"And perhaps you will come to the party for a little while," said Nurse Jane. "I'm sure all the children will be glad to see you, and you may care to nibble a bit of the ice cream we are going to have."

"Ice cream!" cried Uncle Wiggily. "Say no more, if you please! I'll be there."

Then the rabbit gentleman went on over his farm, to see how the beets, carrots, turnips, onions and potatoes were growing, while Miss Fuzzy Wuzzy got ready for the little party.

Uncle Wiggily found some weeds growing in the middle of the onion bed, where they had gone to sleep, but he soon pulled them out and hopped on, now and then leaning on his red, white and blue striped rheumatism crutch that Nurse Jane had gnawed for him out of a cornstalk.

"Well, I think, perhaps, I had better go back and see how the party in the flower garden is coming along." thought Mr. Longears after a while. "It may be they have so much ice cream they don't know what to do with it, and there may be enough left for Grandfather Goosey Gander and me."

So back he hopped to the garden where the flowers grew, and, as he came near the place, he heard shouts and laughter from those at the party.

"You're it!" someone cried.

"No, I tagged you first," laughed another.

"Oh, let's play the jump game," chattered Billie Bushytail, the squirrel boy.

"I think the lollypop game would be better," spoke Susie Littletail.

Then they played both these, as well as other games until some one saw Uncle Wiggily hopping along.

"Oh, now we'll have some fun!" cried the animal children. "We'll have a jolly good time now."

"Easy, easy!" begged Uncle Wiggily, laughing. "You'll break my rheumatism crutch if you're not careful."

Hopping, jumping, flying and walking, the animal children gathered around the rabbit gentleman, for they were glad to have him at their party.

Everything was as delightful as heart could wish, and there was ice cream enough for all, when, all of a sudden, the wind began to blow.

"Oh, I'm afraid it's going to rain!" cried Nurse Jane, who was giving the party.

"Get the umbrellas!" said Sammie Littletail.

"There goes my hair ribbon!" giggled Nannie Wagtail, the little goat girl.

"And mine, too," added Beckie Stubtail, the little bear girl.

"That's all right. "I'll make new ones for you out of the ribbon grass in my garden," said Uncle Wiggily. He was just doing this, when, all at once, down poured the rain, and there were not enough umbrellas for the animal children to get under.

"Oh, what shall we do?" they cried. "We'll get soaking wet!"

"No, you will not," suddenly said Uncle Wiggily. "I can make an umbrella for each of you, so the rain will not wet you in the least. Ready, now!"

Quickly, from the stems of the hollyhock flowers, he picked the blossoms, some red, some white and some pink. A hollyhock blossom is just like an open umbrella, and, when the animal chil-

dren at the party held them upside down over
their heads, the rain drops ran off to the ground,
and no one was wet more than a drop or two,
which did not matter in the least.

Home ran the animal children from Nurse
Jane's party, holding the hollyhock flower umbrellas over their heads, and very thankful they
were to Uncle Wiggily for being so kind to them.

Thus, you see, that flowers are of some use in
this world besides being merely beautiful, though
that is why we all like them. And, if the button
hook doesn't try to pull the gold fish out of the
canary's cage, to play hop-scotch with the hand
organ monkey, I'll tell you next about Uncle
Wiggily and the little turnip.

STORY XVIII

UNCLE WIGGILY AND THE LITTLE TURNIP

"Well, well! I never did see such a little one as you!" exclaimed Uncle Wiggily Longears, the rabbit gentleman, one morning as he walked down to the end of his farm.

"What is it?" asked Nurse Jane Fuzzy Wuzzy, who was washing the breakfast dishes. "Is Squeaky-Eeky, the little cousin mouse, down there, Uncle Wiggily?"

"No, Janie," he answered. "It is a little turnip of whom I am speaking. It is the littlest turnip I ever saw, not much bigger than a hickory nut, but still strong and healthy."

"Maybe it's one that isn't yet ripe," said Nurse Jane.

"Oh, yes, it's ripe," Uncle Wiggily answered. "I just pulled it from the ground, with some others I am going to store in my cellar, besides the carrots and similar vegetables for winter. It is ripe, all right, but such a little turnip! Come and look at it, Janie."

Nurse Jane looked at the little turnip. As Uncle Wiggily had said, it was fully ripe and ready to be pulled. But, oh! it was so small!

"It isn't anything like the big, giant carrot we pulled up yesterday, is it?" asked the muskrat lady.

"I should say not!" laughed Uncle Wiggily.

"Are you going to save such a little turnip?" asked Nurse Jane as she saw Uncle Wiggily putting the tiny one on a pile with some others, of large and regular size.

"Oh, yes, I'll save it," he said. "You never can tell when you might need a little turnip. And now-a-days, with everything so high, and lollypops maybe going to cost two cents a piece, we must save everything."

So Nurse Jane went back to her dishes and Uncle Wiggily walked on over his farm, coming back finally to where he had left the little turnip.

"I wonder if I will find a use for such a little chap as you," said the bunny uncle, speaking out loud and twinkling his nose.

"I'm sure I'm much obliged to you for saving me," spoke the little turnip, which could talk rabbit language as well as understand it. "I want to be useful to you Uncle Wiggily, even if you only put me in the soup, or mash me up with some potatoes for your Thanksgiving dinner."

"Thank you," spoke the bunny rabbit gentleman. "I'm glad I saved you, even if you are small."

"Oh, small things are often useful," said the little turnip. "I'll do my best."

"Well, of all the airs she's giving herself!" sneered one of the big turnips. "If I had my way she wouldn't be on the same farm with us. It's disgraceful!"

"That's what I say!" sniffed another big turnip.

Uncle Wiggily was just thinking of going to look at his cabbage when, all of a sudden, a big alligator, one of the skillery-scalery kind, hopped out from behind a currant bush and cried:

"Not so fast, if you please, Mr. Longears."

"Why not?" asked Uncle Wiggily, for the alligator had caught him by his coat tails. "What do you want with me?"

"I want you to come to dinner with me," spoke the skillery-scalery alligator.

Uncle Wiggily's pink, twinkling nose turned pale. Well did he know what that meant.

"Oh, dear!" exclaimed the bunny. "I don't want to come to dinner with you. I'm afraid you might bite me by mistake, instead of the bread and butter."

"No matter what you're afraid of," snapped the alligator, "come with me!"

He was just going to drag Uncle Wiggily off to his den when, all of a sudden, the little turnip gave a big jump, helped by a puff of wind, and right in the alligator's eye she landed.

"Oh, me! My eye!" cried the 'gator, letting go of Uncle Wiggily. "Oh, a grain of sand is in my eye, and how it hurts! Oh, wow! Oh, I am shedding so many tears I can't see! Oh, double wow! How that sand hurts!"

It wasn't the sand at all, but the little midget turnip, no bigger than the head of a hatpin, which was in the 'gator's eye. And the turnip wriggled around and made the bad creature's eye smart so much and made such a lot of salty tear-water come in it, that he had to run away, and so didn't get Uncle Wiggily after all. So you see the little turnip did some good and late that night she dropped out of the 'gator's eye and was blown back to Uncle Wiggily's farm.

And if the snow shovel can climb out of the coal bin and play tag with the water pipe before they both go to sleep in the ash can, I'll tell you next about Uncle Wiggily and the stones.

STORY XIX

UNCLE WIGGILY AND THE STONES

"Well, where are you going this morning, Uncle Wiggily?" asked Nurse Jane Fuzzy Wuzzy, the muskrat lady housekeeper, as she saw the rabbit gentleman hopping down off the front porch of his hollow stump farm house. "Are you going to dig potatoes, or shell some peas?"

"Well, I don't exactly know," answered the rabbit gentleman. "I am going to take a walk over my farm and see how it looks after the rain," for there had been a shower in the night, and now, as the sun came up, each leaf glistened like forty 'leven million diamonds.

"Well, don't forget to come back for lunch," said Nurse Jane as she went in and closed the door so the flies couldn't buzz around the gas stove. "We are going to have watermelon short cake for lunch."

"Oh, I'll be sure to come," laughed Uncle Wiggily, and then he went on over his farm.

Through the woods and across the fields he went, and pretty soon he came to a place where he had planted some beans.

"They ought to be almost ready to pick now,"

said the bunny gentleman to himself, but my goodness me sakes alive, and some buttered toast! When Mr. Longears looked for the beans he couldn't see one. They had not come up.

"This is funny!" exclaimed the bunny uncle.

"What is funny?" asked a voice suddenly, and at first the bunny was afraid it might be the skillery scalery alligator with the humps on his tail, or the ear-scratching cat. But it was neither, being, in fact, Grandfather Goosey Gander himself.

"What is funny?" asked Grandpa Goosey.

"No beans growing here," said Uncle Wiggily. "I am sure I planted some. It's funny they didn't come up."

Grandpa Goosey flew over the fence and looked at the ground.

"No wonder your beans did not come up," he said.

"Why didn't they?" Uncle Wiggily wanted to know.

"Because there are too many stones in this field," went on Grandpa Goosey. "Why, it is just covered with them! The beans must be all underneath the stones."

"If I took the stones off, would the beans come up?" asked the bunny gentleman.

"Of course they would," spoke Grandpa Goosey.

"Then off come the stones!" cried Uncle Wiggily, and he began throwing them off his field into a little brook nearby, which already had many stones in it, but which did not mind having more.

"I'll help you," said Grandpa Goosey, and he, too, began tossing away the stones.

But the rabbit gentleman and the goose grandpa had tossed only a few stones when their backs began to ache, for they were not boys any longer, you know, though they acted so sometimes.

"Oh, dear!" cried Uncle Wiggily. "It will take us a year to clear this field of stones. There are so many!"

"There are quite a lot," said Grandpa Goosey sadly. "But if we don't get rid of the stones the beans will not grow."

Uncle Wiggily looked at the hundreds and thousands of stones. Then he suddenly cried, with a twinkle of his nose:

"Ha! I know what to do. I have a plan to get rid of these stones very easily."

"How?" asked Grandpa Goosey.

"I'll show you in a minute. Just you stay here and, when you hear me coming back, you begin throwing stones, easy like so as not to strain your wing."

"Well," said Grandpa Goosey, wiping his yellow bill on a blade of green grass, "I don't know what your plan is, but I'll do as you say. Hop along!"

So Uncle Wiggily hopped along, his eyes twinkling as well as his nose. Pretty soon he met Sammie Littletail, the rabbit boy.

"Sammie, are you a good stone thrower?" asked the bunny uncle.

"Fine!" cried Sammie. "The best ever!"

"Come with me," said Uncle Wiggily, mysterious like.

He went along a little farther and met Johnnie and Billie Bushytail, the two squirrels.

"Are you good stone throwers?" he asked them.

"Dandy!" they chattered.

"Come with me!" invited the bunny uncle. And, in the same way, he got Jackie and Peetie Bow Wow, the puppies, and Billie Wagtail, the goat, and many other animal boys. Then he took them to the stony field.

"Ahem!" cried Uncle Wiggily out loud, to let Grandpa Goosey know he was coming, with the animal boys. At once the goose gentleman began throwing stones.

"Ha!" cried Uncle Wiggily, innocent like.

"There is some one throwing stones out of my field. He seems to be a good thrower, too. I wonder if any of you boys can beat him?"

"I can!" cried Sammie. "And I—and I!" cried the other animal chaps. "We can beat him throwing stones!"

Down into the stony field they scampered, and each one began throwing stones out of it into the brook, trying to beat Grandpa Goosey and each other. In a little while, not a stone was left in the field and the beans could come up as easy as pie.

"My! My!" cried Uncle Wiggily, rubbing his eyes as he saw all the stones gone and without any trouble on his part at all. "You animal chaps are certainly good throwers. I guess I'll have to give you each an ice cream cone."

And he did, and Sammie and the others wondered why Uncle Wiggily and Grandpa Goosey laughed so. Do you know?

Anyhow, this teaches us that there are more ways of eating pie than with a fork. And, if the lollypop doesn't fall off the stick and splash into the mulberry jam when they pass each other in the salt cellar, I'll tell you next about Uncle Wiggily and the hay.

STORY XX

UNCLE WIGGILY AND THE HAY

"Well, there is no use in talking," said the bad old ear-scratching cat, as he sat under a tree one morning and looked first at the unpleasant tail-pulling monkey, and then at the nose-pinching baboon. "There is no use at all in talking!"

"No, and not much use doing anything else, either," said the chimp, as I call the chimpanzee for short. "We haven't been able to catch him."

"I presume you are conversing about Uncle Wiggily Longears; are you not?" spoke the baboon, formal like and disdainful.

"I am," said the ear-scratching cat. "All the things we did to catch him didn't amount to a hill of the beans he grows on his farm. We might as well quit."

"Oh, don't say that!" cried the bab, which is short for baboon.

"What can we do?" asked the cat.

"Well, we all tried separately to catch him," went on the chimpanzee, "speaking of the different times they had tried to capture the bunny, "suppose we try now together. All three of us will go as one and get him. Then we can scratch

106

his ears, pinch his nose and pull his tail as much
as we like and make up for lost time."

"All right, I'm willing to try," spoke the cat,
"but how is it to be done?"

"I'll tell you," said the baboon. "I was around
Uncle Wiggily's hollow stump farm house the
other day, and I heard him say he was going soon
to cut his hay and put it in the barn. We'll just
watch from behind the fence until he does that
and then we'll come up behind him, when he's
riding in on the load of hay. We'll all get hold
together, pull him off and then we'll have him."

"Good!" meauowed the cat, though, I, myself,
call it bad. "That's how we'll get him! Come
on, let's keep watch and see when he goes after
the hay."

So the three bad creatures made ready to get
our Uncle Wiggily. But let us wait and see how
he fools them, that is, providing my plans work
out right and he does. Let us see, as they say in
books.

It was not long after this that Uncle Wiggily
took a walk across his farm. He came to the field
where grew the hay and he said:

"Yes, I must soon cut this and haul it into my
barn ready for winter, though cold weather is
still far off, I hope. My hay is ready to cut. I
must see my friends and have them help me."

So Uncle Wiggily called his friends together, especially an old swordfish whom he had met while on his vacation at the seashore, and the swordfish, with his long, sharp nose, promised to cut the hay, which he did as well as you could have done it with a lawn mower.

"And now to haul the hay into the barn," said Uncle Wiggily.

"You may have my express wagon for that," kindly said Sammie Littletail, the rabbit boy.

"And with my long, sharp horns, I'll pitch the hay up on the wagon for you," said the Cow Who Jumped Over the Moon. "For my horns are like a pitchfork."

"Thank you," said Uncle Wiggily.

"And I'll haul into the barn for you the wagon load of hay," said Gup, the kind old horse, for he was very strong.

"Thank you all, very kindly," spoke Uncle Wiggily. Then, with his friends, including the swordfish, he went out to the hay field.

"Now's our chance!" exclaimed the bad cat, who was on the watch with the monkey and baboon.

And, softly, very softly, they went on after Uncle Wiggily, intending to get him this time sure.

The swordfish cut the hay, as I have told you.

Then it was gathered into piles all over the field.

"Now watch me toss it up on the wagon!" cried the Moon-Cow, as I call her for short.

She stuck her horns in a pile of fodder, gave a toss of her head, and up on the wagon went the hay. Uncle Wiggily stood on the wagon to spread out the hay evenly as the Moon-Cow tossed it up.

Higher and higher on the wagon the hay was piled, and Gup, the kind horse, who was to pull the wagon to the barn, stood waiting, eating the wisps of hay that fell off to the ground.

"Well, I guess we'll call this a load," said Uncle Wiggily, after a bit. "Get up, Gup!"

So Gup started off and the bad ear-scratching cat said to the chimpanzee and baboon:

"Come on! Now's our chance!"

After the hay wagon, on top of which rode Uncle Wiggily, they went. Oh, how sure they were that they were going to catch the bunny uncle! But are they? Just watch!

"Now all together!" cried the cat.

The three of them reached up to pull the hay wagon, Uncle Wiggily, hay and all head over heels, when, all of a sudden, the front wheels struck a stone. Before Gup could stop it, the wagon tilted up in the air, the front end going high and the back end low. Off slid the load of hay, right on top of the bad cat, the worse baboon and the worst chimpanzee. They were covered out of sight, but, as for Uncle Wiggily, he just stayed right on top of the soft hay, and sat there the same as if he were on a soft cushion, so he wasn't hurt at all.

But the three bad creatures were away down under the hay that had slid off the wagon, and the dust got up their noses and the hay tickled them and they sneezed and choked and coughed, and had a dreadful time. They crawled out as fast as they could, and ran away.

"My goodness!" cried Uncle Wiggily as he saw them go. "I didn't know they were any-where around." And I guess the three bad ones wished they hadn't been.

Then the cow and Gup loaded the hay back on the wagon again and all was well. So Uncle Wiggily got away again, you see, and, if the fire shovel doesn't burn its handle when it takes the ashes out for a trolley ride, I'll tell you next about Uncle Wiggily and the groundhog.

STORY XXI

UNCLE WIGGILY AND THE GROUNDHOG

"Oh, Uncle Wiggily! Uncle Wiggily! Hurry up!" called Billie Bushytail, the squirrel boy, one morning as he ran over to the hollow stump farm house where the rabbit gentleman lived with Nurse Jane Fuzzy Wuzzy, the muskrat lady.

"What's the matter?" the bunny uncle wanted to know. "Has your brother Johnnie swallowed a nut down his wrong throat, or is Mother Goose taking my automobile up in the sky to sweep away the cobwebs?"

"Neither one," answered Billie, who was so excited that his tail went up and down just like a pump handle. "But there's a great big animal over in one of your farm-fields, Uncle Wiggily," he went on. "I just saw him as I ran past on the fence. Oh! He's awful big! You ought to go drive him out, or he may eat up all your cabbages, potatoes and onions."

"I don't much care if he does eat the onions," said Uncle Wiggily, with a laugh, "for I don't like them myself. Still, if some big animal is on my farm—was it a bear?" he suddenly asked Billie.

111

"No, it wasn't big enough for a bear," the little squirrel boy said.

"Was it the skillery-scalery alligator?" asked the bunny man.

"No, and it didn't seem to be the fox, either, nor yet the tail-pulling chimpanzee nor even the ear-scratching cat," went on Billie.

"I'll go see what it is," said the brave rabbit gentleman. He took a pop gun he had bought for his little nephew, Sammie Littletail, and, with talcum powder to put in it to shoot, and some beans for bullets, off he started.

"Don't you want to come along, Billie?" he asked.

"Oh, no, thank you. I——think I hear my mother calling me—she wants me," spoke the chattering squirrel chap, sort of diffident—and not at all eager like.

"Well, I'll go myself," said Uncle Wiggily, sort of smiling at Billie.

The rabbit man came to a big field of clover on his farm, and, looking over down among the green leaves he saw some animal sitting near a stone.

"Ha! Billie was right! There is some one there!" exclaimed Uncle Wiggily to himself. "This must never be! I am not running an animal farm."

Then, getting behind the fence, he loaded his popgun with the sweet-smelling talcum powder, and, aiming it at the animal, cried:

"Excuse me, but this is my farm! I don't want to be cross or impolite, but you must go away and not eat any of my clover."

"Oh, I must, eh?" cried the strange animal, and then, sitting up on its hind legs, it looked at Uncle Wiggily as it asked: "Do you know who I am?"

"I can't help who you are," said Uncle Wiggily. "You must get out of my field."

"I am the groundhog," was the answer, "and I must eat clover. All groundhogs do that. If I didn't eat clover, I couldn't be a groundhog— I'd have to be a bad cat or a dog or a fox, or even—"

"Oh, say no more!" cried Uncle Wiggily, sort of tying his ears in a knot. "I did not know you were a groundhog. And you are some relation, I suppose, to Grunter, Squeaker and Twisty-tail, the pigs, who belong to Mother Goose."

"Yes, I'm their thirty-second cousin," said the groundhog.

"And I am very sorry I ordered you out of my field. You may stay in it as long as you please and eat as much clover as you like," spoke Uncle Wiggily.

"Thank you," said the groundhog, as he went on eating. "Come and see me some time. I live right over there," and he pointed to a big hole in the ground, almost as large as a water pail.

"I will come to see you," promised Uncle Wiggily. And he was to make a visit much sooner than he expected.

For a little while the rabbit gentleman stood by the fence, watching the groundhog eat the clover, and Uncle Wiggily was glad there was plenty of it on his farm.

"Well," said the bunny uncle after a while, "I guess I might as well leave my popgun with the talcum powder and bean bullets here, while I look over the rest of my fields."

So he did, hopping along on his way, but he had not traveled very far before, all of a sudden, out from behind a stump jumped the bad old ear-scratching cat.

"Wow! Meaouw!" howled the cat. "Now I have you for sure! You can't get away from me this time!"

"Oh, can't I? Well, we'll see," said Uncle Wiggily. Away he ran, but the cat ran after him, and the bad creature went so much faster than the bunny that Mr. Longears soon saw he could not get away.

"Oh, if I had only thought to bring the popgun," he said, "I could shoot the cat. Or if I only had time to stop and dig a hole I could crawl in it and hide. But I can do neither. Oh, dear! I guess I'm caught!"

Then, all at once, the bunny uncle heard a voice calling:

"Jump down in my house, Uncle Wiggily. There you will be safe from the cat. Here's the hole—jump in," and there stood the clover-eating groundhog, pointing to his underground house.

Down into this jumped Uncle Wiggily, with the groundhog following after and closing the stone front door so the cat could not get down.

"Fooled again!" yowled the bad creature, lashing its tail when it found the rabbit was gone. But Uncle Wiggily was safe in the hole, and he was very glad he had let the groundhog stay on his farm to eat clover. And, when the cat ran away, the bunny uncle could come out of the hole and go safely to his farm house bungalow.

So, if the clothespin doesn't hide in the peach basket, to get away from the wringer, which might pinch its nose, I'll tell you next about Uncle Wiggily and the mustard.

STORY XXII

UNCLE WIGGILY AND THE MUSTARD

"Uncle Wiggily, does any mustard grow on your farm?" asked Nurse Jane Fuzzy Wuzzy, the muskrat lady house-keeper one day, as she saw the rabbit gentleman putting on his tall silk hat to hop across the fields, where he had planted many things.

"Mustard?" he exclaimed. "Why, yes, I think so. I'll look," and he opened a little book in which he had written the names of all the seeds he had planted on his farm.

"Hum!" he went on, thoughtful like. "Let's see now—muskmellon, marshmallow candy, mince pies. Ah, yes, here we are. Mustard! It's in the green meadow over by the brook. Do you want some mustard, Nurse Jane?"

"I would like a little," said she. "I am making some mustard pickles and the mustard on your farm is much better than any I could get at the store."

"Oh, it's ever so much better!" cried the bunny uncle. "I'll bring you some when I come back, after tying knots in the string beans. They are

116

slipping off the poles, and I must fasten them on."

"Well, don't forget the mustard!" cried the muskrat lady, playfully shaking her tail at the bunny uncle, who hopped on, his pink nose twinkling in the sun like a strawberry on top of an orange shortcake.

On and over his farm went the rabbit gentleman, and pretty soon he came to where the beans grew. Some of them needed tying up on the poles, and, after he had done this, Uncle Wiggily started back for the hollow stump farm house.

He had not gone very far before he thought about the mustard he had promised to bring to Nurse Jane.

"I'll hop over to the green brook-meadow and pick some for her," he said.

The mustard bush was a very big one, though the plant itself has very little seeds, and soon Uncle Wiggily had picked enough of them for Nurse Jane. He wrapped the mustard seeds in a green leaf of the plant and put the little package in the top of his tall silk hat.

The old rabbit gentleman walked a little farther across his farm, and then he thought it was time to go back to the hollow stump, for he was getting hungry. He had not hopped very far, however, before he heard a rustling in the bushes near him, and he saw the bush move, and before Uncle Wiggily could do or say anything out popped the bad old ear-scratching cat.

"Ah, ha! Oh, ho!" yowled the cat. "We meet again, I see," and he screwed up his whiskers in such a funny way that Uncle Wiggily wanted to laugh, and he would have done it, too, only he was afraid the cat would not like it. "We meet again, you see," the unpleasant creature went on.

"Yes," said Uncle Wiggily slowly and sadly, "we do, but I am not any the happier for it."

"No, but think how happy I am!" exclaimed the cat. "I have ears to scratch now. Oh, such nice, big, long ears," and the cat looked at the flipping, flopping ones of the rabbit gentleman, and put out his sharp claws, sort as if he were practicing his music lesson on the piano, that cat did. But what he really was doing was practicing for scratching Uncle Wiggily's ears.

"Oh, please let me go!" begged the bunny uncle, as the cat suddenly put out one paw and caught him fast by the edge of his coat.

"Oh, no, I shan't let you go!" said the cat. "You are coming with me. I have some little kittens and I wish to teach them ear-scratching, so you are very much needed. Come with me to my den."

"Please don't!" begged the rabbit again.

"Yes, I shall!" yowled the cat, and away he led poor Mr. Longears, who wished, very much indeed, that he had tiny little ears, like a canary bird, for then the cat couldn't have seen them to scratch them.

Uncle Wiggily looked all around for some one to help him, but he saw no one. There was not a policeman dog in sight to scare away that cat, and it looked as though Uncle Wiggily was in for a bad time.

And then, all of a sudden, he saw, quite a long way off, Mrs. Wibblewobble, the duck lady.

"Oh, Mrs. Wibblewobble, how do you do!" cried the bunny, and then, acting politely as he always did, he took off his tall silk hat and made a bow. Mrs. Wibblewobble was too far off to see the bow or help the rabbit, but when Uncle Wiggily took off his hat out fell the leaf full of hot mustard seeds. Out on the ground it fell.

"Ah, ha! What is this?" cried the cat. "Something good to eat, I'm sure!"

"Don't take that! It's for Nurse Jane," said Uncle Wiggily. "She is going to make—"

"She is going to make nothing of this!" impolitely interrupted the cat, "for I am going to eat it!" With that he made a bite into the leaf-full of mustard seeds and then—

Well, I guess you know what happened.

"Oh, wow!" yelled the cat. "Oh, double wow and a trolley transfer on another one! Oh, mush cakes and fish balls! Oh!"

And with that, his mouth burning like fire, that bad cat ran away to get a drink of ice water, and so he didn't scratch our Uncle Wiggily after all.

"My! It's a good thing I had that mustard," said the bunny, as he went back to get some more seeds for Nurse Jane's pickles. And then he hopped safely home to dinner.

And if the bluebird doesn't turn red when it sees the gold fish trying to swim with the cracker dust in the bread box, I'll tell you next about Uncle Wiggily and the chickweed.

STORY XXIII

UNCLE WIGGILY AND THE CHICKWEED

Sammie Littletail, the rabbit boy, was one day taking a hop, skip and a jump over the farm of Uncle Wiggily Longears, the bunny gentleman, about whom I have told you so many stories.

"My! Uncle Wiggily certainly has a nice farm," said Sammie, as he looked at the popcorn and baked beans and the succotash and the tomato salad and eggplants, to say nothing of the carrots and lettuce, growing in the fields. The horse-radish was running toward the beans which were climbing up poles just like the man in the circus, and the strong onions were making the potatoes blink their eyes, so they couldn't talk to the corn, which was listening with all its ears.

Sammie saw some little, green, shiny leaves, with tiny flowers among them, growing close to the ground.

"Oh, I wonder what that plant is?" exclaimed the rabbit boy.

"I am the chickweed, if you please," was the cheerful answer.

"Chickweed!" cried Sammie. "Say no more. I must tell Uncle Wiggily about this."

Away hopped the rabbit boy to where the bunny uncle was sitting on the front porch of the hollow stump farm house.

"Oh, Uncle Wiggily," cried Sammie. "What do you think I found growing on your farm just now?"

"Well, I'm sure I don't know," answered the old rabbit gentleman. "I hope the old skillery-scalery alligator hasn't been planting moth balls, so a lot of butterflies will hatch out."

"No, it isn't like that," Sammie said. "It's a plant that will grow little chickens. Come and see it quick, before it goes away."

"A plant that grows little chickens!" Uncle Wiggily cried. "That is very strange. I did not know I had that kind on my farm. Somebody must have been planting eggs. I'll come with you right away, Sammie."

So the old rabbit gentleman, taking his red, white and blue striped rheumatism crutch down off the porch railing, where it was having a rest, started off with Sammie across the farm.

"There it is, Uncle Wiggily!" cried Sammie, pointing to the green leaves growing down in a corner by the fence. "There is the plant that will make little chickens. Let's stay here until some hatch out. Won't it be funny to see little chickens come out from under the green leaves instead of out of egg shells?"

"It certainly will, Sammie," laughed Uncle Wiggily. "But it never will happen. Ho! Ha! Ha! Also, ho! ho!"

"Why, what is the matter?" asked Sammie, for his rabbit uncle was now laughing very hard. "Can't chickens grow out of this plant?"

"No, indeed, Sammie, my boy," answered the rabbit gentleman. "It is true that the name of these green leaves is chick, but it is chickweed, and not a plant which will turn into little chickens. It is only a weed, so I must pull it up and cut it down or it will spoil my farm," and Uncle Wiggily raised his crutch, as though he would beat the chickweed all to pieces.

"Oh, please don't spoil us!" begged the chickweed flowers and leaves. "It is true we are neither a fruit nor a vegetable, but if you let us grow on your farm we may be able to do some freind of yours a favor. Let us stay."

Now Uncle Wiggily had the kindest heart in the world, so when he heard the chickweed say this he scratched his whiskers, twinkled his pink nose, and, wobbling his ears, said:

"Well, I suppose I'll have to. But, dear me! If this keeps on I'll have nothing but weeds on my farm. However, I'll let you grow this time. But don't do it again!"

So the chickweed promised it wouldn't, and Uncle Wiggily and Sammie went on over the farm. After a while Sammie went to the lollypop store to get an ice cream cone, and the rabbit gentleman hopped along to his hollow stump house.

No sooner had he gotten there than he saw Nurse Jane Fuzzy Wuzzy, the muskrat lady housekeeper, running up and down on the porch, tying her tail in hard knots and quickly taking them out again.

"Why, whatever is the matter, Jane?" asked the rabbit.

"Oh, matter enough!" she cried. "Charlie, the little chicken boy of Mrs. Cluck-Cluck, the hen lady, is very ill. We have sent for Dr. Possum, but he isn't in his office. Mrs. Cluck-Cluck says if she could only find some chickweed for Charlie he would soon be better without having the doctor."

"Chickweed!" cried Uncle Wiggily. "Say no more! I know where some is and I'll get it at once." Then, jumping into his automobile and sprinkling pepper on the bologna sausage tires to make them go faster, he soon rode to that part of his farm where the chickweed grew.

"Quick!" cried the bunny uncle. "I need some of your leaves to make Charlie Chick better. May I take some?"

"As many as you like," said the kind chickweed. "We are glad to help!"

Then Uncle Wiggily plucked some leaves and blossoms, and when Mrs. Cluck-Cluck had made a tea of them, and Charlie had sipped it, he was all well again.

"Oh, I'm so glad I didn't pull up that chickweed on my farm," said Uncle Wiggily that night. "It is good, even if it isn't a fruit or vegetable."

So this teaches us that everything has some use in this world, even mosquitoes, though please don't ask me what good they are. And if the motorcycle doesn't turn into a hand organ and sew the monkey's tail fast to the jitney bus, I'll tell you next about Uncle Wiggily and the shortcake.

STORY XXIV

UNCLE WIGGILY AND THE SHORTCAKE

"Do you know what we are going to have for supper tonight, Nurse Jane?" asked Uncle Wiggily Longears, the rabbit gentleman, as he saw his muskrat lady housekeeper clearing off the table after lunch one day.

"Why, yes, seeing that I have to cook it, of course, I know what we are going to have for supper," she answered with a laugh. "We are going to have stewed carrots, fried parsnips, a bit of lettuce salad and cucumber pancake.

"Something else!" laughed Uncle Wiggily, making his rheumatism crutch dance a jig on the floor. "We are going to have something else."

"Is it ice cream?" asked Nurse Jane. "Are you going to bring some ice cream home for dessert?"

"Not exactly," Uncle Wiggily answered. "But it is almost at nice. It's going to be strawberry shortcake."

"Strawberry shortcake!" cried Nurse Jane. "How are you going to buy that at the five and ten cent store?"

"I didn't say I was going to buy it," laughed

the bunny uncle, his pink nose twinkling faster than ever. "You are going to make the cake."

"I?" asked Nurse Jane, sort of flustered like. "Pray tell how I can make a strawberry short-cake when I have no berries!"

"But you shall have them," Uncle Wiggily spoke. "Some lovely strawberies grow on my farm, and I am now going over to pick a basket-ful. When I come back with them you can make the cake."

"Fine!" cried Nurse Jane. "I'll be baking the cake part while you're after the berries, since they do not need to be baked. Hurry along, Wiggily! Speaking of strawberries makes me hungry."

"I'll go for them at once," said the bunny uncle, and away he started hopping, skipping and jumping over the fields and woods of his farm, now and then leaning on his red, white and blue striped rheumatism crutch that Nurse Jane had gnawed for him out of a sugar cane—excuse me, I mean a corn stalk.

It was a pleasant summer day, with the sun brightly shining, and Uncle Wiggily did not have to hurry, as it would not be time for supper until several hours later. So he took his time, now and then stopping to look at something growing on his farm.

By-and-by he came to the strawberry patch, and there he saw the bright red berries gleaming like stars down in the green leaves.

"Oh, it seems too bad to pick you and take you out of your nice, green leafy bed," said the bunny uncle, "but I know you would rather go into a strawberry shortcake for Nurse Jane and me than be out here all alone—wouldn't you?"

"Indeed, we would!" said the strawberries all together in a sort of ice cream soda voice.

So Uncle Wiggily began to pick them, putting them in the basket he had brought with him on his paw.

In a little while it was nearly full, and he thought, as he now had enough of the red berries, that he would go back to his hollow stump farm house with them, to let Nurse Jane put them to sleep in the cake.

"Yes, I'll go now," said Uncle Wiggily, speaking out loud, as he sometimes did in talking to himself.

"Oh, no, you shan't" suddenly exclaimed a harsh voice.

"Shan't what?" Uncle Wiggily asked.

"You shan't go away now and leave me like this. I want you to come with me." And there, on the outside of the strawberry bed, stood the bad old fox.

"Oh, dear!" sadly said the bunny uncle. "I wish you had stayed away until I got safely home."

"Oh, ho! But I don't!" snarled the fox. "If I had stayed away I would have had no supper to-night. For you are coming to supper with me. We are going to have a good time together."

"I guess you'll have all the good time," went on Mr. Longears, for well he knew what the fox would do to him—make a stew of him without a doubt.

"Well, come along now," said the fox, "I'm getting hungry for my supper."

"Oh, if you are hungry, won't you have some of these?" asked Uncle Wiggily, politely holding out his basket on his paw.

"Have some of what?" asked the fox.

"Strawberries," said the bunny uncle. Do have some. They will make you feel less hungry," for Uncle Wiggily thought if the fox ate enough strawberries he would not want a rabbit stew for supper."

"Well, I'll try just one," said the fox, and taking a ripe, red strawberry from the bunny gentleman's basket in his paw the hungry fox squeezed the berry so hard that the red juice ran all over his leg and paw, and he cried:

"Oh what a trick! What a trick! You fooled

me. You didn't give me a strawberry at all!
You gave me a knife and I have cut myself. I
am bleeding to death! Oh, dear! This is terrible.
I must run to the doctor's at once. Oh, dear!"

And, seeing the red strawberry juice on his
paw, and thinking he was cut, when he wasn't at
all, away ran the fox, leaving Uncle Wiggily
safely there with the berries for the shortcake.

"Well, that was getting off easy," said Mr.
Longears, with a smile, as he hopped on home.
"I did not believe the fox was so easily scared."

Then the bunny gentleman and Nurse Jane
had a fine strawberry shortcake for supper, and
if the cricket doesn't play his chirping fiddle so
loudly that he scares the lightning bug out of the
moving pictures, I'll tell you next about Uncle
Wiggily and the stump.

STORY XXV

UNCLE WIGGILY AND THE STUMP

"Bang! Bang! Bangity-bang-bang!"

That is what Uncle Wiggily Longears, the rabbit gentleman, heard one morning as he awakened in his hollow stump farm house and looked out of the window.

"Hello! What's that?" he cried, sitting up in bed and stretching his whiskers. "Is the roof falling in, or is some hunter man shooting at my chimney?"

"Neither one," answered Nurse Jane Fuzzy Wuzzy, the muskrat lady housekeeper, who was down in the kitchen making the fried eggs dance in the pan for the rabbit gentleman's breakfast. "Don't you know what day it is?" she asked.

"Why, it's Monday, isn't it?" asked the bunny uncle.

"Yes, but it is also the Fourth of July," answered the muskrat lady. "And the noise you hear is—"

"Ha! I know now!" cried Uncle Wiggily, jumping out of bed. "Of course! It's the fire-crackers, the torpedoes and the paper caps being

131

shot off by the animal boys and girls, because they are go glad there is no more school.   Hip! Hip! Hurray!" he shouted, dancing around on his red, white and blue striped rheumatism crutch, which Nurse Jane had gnawed for him out of a cornstalk.

"I'm going to celebrate, too!" went on the rabbit gentleman.   "I'm going to be glad I'm living under the Stars and Stripes, and I'm going to make a noise, too!"

"What are you going to do?" asked Nurse Jane.

"Blow up a stump," replied the bunny.   "On my farm are a lot of old, big, black stumps, and where they are stuck in the ground nothing will grow.

"I'll make some holes in them, put powder in the holes and touch a match to it.   The powder will blow the stump all to pieces, and it will make a big noise.   So I'll have my Fourth of July and, at the same time, be joyful and glad that I live in the home of the free and the land of the brave."

"Good for you!" cried Nurse Jane, waving her tail, as she had no flag, just then, to flutter.

So the animal children—Sammie and Susie Littletail, Johnnie and Billie Bushtail, Lulu Alice and Jimmie Wibblewobble, who were ducks, and Jackie and Peetie Bow Wow, the puppies, to say nothing of Nannie and Billie Wagtail, the goats, had their Fourth of July fun.

In those days it was all right for the rabbits, squirrels, guinea pigs, little bears, ducks and goats to shoot firecrackers as much as they liked, for the things they shot were only very, very little pieces of fireworks. But now it is better for you real boys and girls to go to a picnic, or drink pink lemonade, or something like that, instead of burning yourself or hurting yourself with powder.

So there was a bang-up time in animal land, and when Uncle Wiggily had put some gunpowder in his valise, after he had eaten his breakfast, over the fields he went to see where the old stumps were in the way on his farm.

With an ice pick the rabbit gentleman made a hole in one stump. Into the hole he poured some powder, and on top of the powder he put a firecracker string, which will burn slowly, and set off the black stuff that makes such a noise.

"I'll have a little Fourth of July all by myself," said Uncle Wiggily, as he lighted the firecracker string, and then off he hopped to be out of the way when the explosion came. He sat down at a safe distance and, while he was waiting, all of a sudden, out from the woods came the bad old skillery-scallery alligator with the double-jointed tail.

Right down on the stump sat the 'gator, and, with a broad smile, he said:

"Ah, ha! At last I have you, Uncle Wiggily. Don't you dare run away from me or I'll throw stones at you and tickle you so in the ribs that you'll turn a somersault, and I'll have you anyhow. Now let me see——"

"Excuse me!" suddenly exclaimed Uncle Wiggily. "But would mind getting off that stump?"

"Get off the stump? I certainly will not!" barked the alligator, almost like a toy dog. "I see what you want. You want me to slip off, and hurt my legs so I can't chase you. But I'll do nothing of the sort. I'll just stay here until I get ready to take you away with me and then——"

"Please get off the stump!" politely begged the rabbit, for well he knew what was going to happen. "Please get off. If you don't——"

But Uncle Wiggily couldn't say it. The firecracker string was smoking, and the spark was getting nearer and nearer to the powder, when, all of a sudden there was a big noise. "Bang!" The stump blew all to pieces. Up in the air, head over heels went the alligator, turning somersault after peppersault, and, as he sailed toward the sky, he cried:

"Oh, safety pins! Why didn't you tell me this was going to happen?"

"I tried to," spoke Uncle Wiggily, "but you would not listen." Then the alligator sailed far, far away, being blown up with Uncle Wiggily's gunpowder stump, and he didn't come down for a long while. But it served him right, I think.

"Oh, Uncle Wiggily is having a Fourth of July!" cried all the animal children when they heard the stump explosion. "Was that a balloon you sent up?" they asked.

"No, that was a flying alligator," said the bunny uncle laughing, and twinkling his pink nose. "He didn't like my stump, so away he flew." Then the Fourth of July fun went on louder than ever, and most jollily.

And if the sidewalk flag stone doesn't wave itself in the air and trip up the postman when he brings a letter to the wax doll, I'll tell you next about Uncle Wiggily and the lion.

STORY XXVI

UNCLE WIGGILY AND THE LION

Uncle Wiggily Longears, the nice rabbit gentleman, was walking down the road one day, going over to a far-distant part of his farm, when, just as he passed the hollow stump school, which would soon close for the summer, he saw, coming out, Susie Littletail, the rabbit girl. Susie had her books under her paw and she was smiling and happy.

"Why do you come out of school, when none of the other animal boys and girls are coming from their classes?" Uncle Wiggily wanted to know.

"Because I finished my lessons," answered Susie. "The lady mouse teacher said I could come home, even if it is early. You see it is examination time, but I am all over mine."

"I hope you passed," went on the bunny uncle.

"I hope so, too," spoke Susie, bending her ears down in a polite bow. "Where are you going?" she asked.

"Over to see how the carrots are growing on my farm," said Mr. Longears. "Don't you want to come with me?"

Uncle Wiggily and the Lion

"Indeed I do!" exclaimed Susie, happy-h. and pleased. She always liked to go anywhere with Uncle Wiggily. So the bunny gentleman and the rabbit girl went along, holding paws, and pretty soon Susie saw something like a green tassel growing out of the ground.

"Oh, how pretty!" she cried. "I will take that home for my hat." And, before Uncle Wiggily could stop her she had pulled up the green thing. On the end was a long, yellow thing, like an ice cream cone, with a sharp point, and before she knew it Susie had pricked herself on her paw with the sharp end.

"Ouch!" she cried. "Your carrots are sharp, just like spears or arrows, Uncle Wiggily."

"Yes, I guess they are," said the bunny man. "You must be careful, Susie."

"I didn't mean to pull up the carrot," went on the little animal girl. "The green top looked just like a tassel, or plume for my hat."

"Oh, take all the carrots you want, only don't stick yourself with them," spoke Uncle Wiggily.

So Susie carried the carrot with her books, and she and Uncle Wiggily went on over the farm.

The carrots were growing very nicely and soon Uncle Wiggily came to where he had planted some beans. They, too, were doing well. Susie picked one of the green beans, and wanted to see what was inside, she broke it open. But it did not easily come apart, being held together by a sort of green cord.

"Oh, Uncle Wiggily!" cried Susie. "What makes the pieces of bean tied together this way?"

"Those are string beans," Uncle Wiggily said, with a laugh. "There is a string on each side of every bean and this string holds them together. When Nurse Jane Fuzzy Wuzzy cooks the beans she has to take off the strings."

"I see," said Susie, and she broke another bean and pulled off the string, while Uncle Wiggily hoed the dirt up around the roots of the corn, making a little hill.

While the rabbit gentleman was doing this Susie looked around for something to play with. At first she could see nothing, but after a while she found a cob, off which the kernels of corn had been shelled.

"Oh, I shall make me a little corncob doll," she said to herself, looking over to see how much longer Uncle Wiggily would be hoeing the corn. He had a number of hills yet to make.

"I'll go over in the corn field and get some silk from the ears of corn to make a dress for my corncob doll," said Susie. "Then I'll have some fun."

She laid down her books and went over to

where the green corn grew. Susie was just taking some of the long, stringy silk, when, happening to look over in the fence corner, she saw something that made her heart beat very fast.

For there, all curled up and asleep, was a big lion. He had gotten away from the circus and had run to hide on Uncle Wiggily's farm.

"Oh, my!" whispered Susie to herself. "What a big lion! If he sees Uncle Wiggily, maybe he'll bite him or carry him off to his cage in the circus," thought the little rabbit girl. "What can I do to save Uncle Wiggily? If I could only tie that lion up so he could not get loose, then he couldn't hurt Uncle Wiggily.

"Ah, ha! I have it! The strong strings from the string beans! I'll tie the lion with them!" Susie said.

Without saying anything to Uncle Wiggily, and not waking up the lion, Susie pulled a lot of strings from the beans These she tied together into a strong rope, and then brave Susie very softly and gently fastened the lion's legs so he could not get up and run.

When she was all finished and the lion was still asleep, Susie went over and told Uncle Wiggily what she had done. And she took with her the sharp-pointed carrot with which to tickle the ribs of any other circus animals that might be on the farm.

"What! You tied up a lion with strings from the beans; did you?" cried the bunny uncle. "Why, that's just fine! I could have done no better myself."

Then with the carrot spear to be used in case anything happened, Uncle Wiggily went with Susie to look at the string-bean-tied-sleeping lion. And the big fellow never woke up until the circus man, later that day, came to put him back in his cage. The circus man took the bean strings off the lion's legs.

"So Susie Littletail tied me up, did she?" said the lion when he was back in his cage. "Well, she needn't have bothered, for I wouldn't have bitten her or Uncle Wiggily, either, not for 1,000,000 popcorn balls."

Thus everything came out all right, you see, and if the teaspoon holder doesn't grab the milk pitcher so tightly that the lemon squeezer has to help pull it loose, I'll tell you next about Uncle Wiggily and the hammocks.

STORY XXVII

UNCLE WIGGILY AND THE HAMMOCKS

"Well, well! What's this?" exclaimed Uncle Wiggily Longears, the rabbit gentleman, as he came down to breakfast in his hollow stump farm house one morning, and found on the table nothing to eat. "What's the matter?"

"Oh, are you down so soon?" asked Nurse Jane Fuzzy Wuzzy, the muskrat lady housekeeper, coming in from the side porch like a policeman, with her tail draped over her paw, the way a June bride carries her train of crepe de sneeze or whatever it is brides wear.

"What's the matter with breakfast?" asked the bunny uncle. "I am very hungry this morning."

"Oh, I beg your pardon," Nurse Jane made answer. "But I was so busy thinking about them that I forgot all about your meal. I'll get it ready at once. Do you think they will fit here?"

"Fit here? What fit here? What were you so busy thinking about?" asked Uncle Wiggily.

"The hammocks," answered Nurse Jane. "You see I bought two new ones up at the five and ten cent store the other day, and I thought it would

141

be nice if you would put them up on this side porch—one for you and one for me."

"Fine!" cried the bunny uncle. "I'll do it at once. Where are the hammocks?"

"They just came," answered Nurse Jane. "I'll take them out of the bundle and then I'll get your breakfast."

"And while you're getting breakfast I'll be putting up the hammocks," said the bunny gentleman.

So Nurse Jane, after opening the five and ten cent store bundle, went in to let the breakfast eggs play tag in the hot water, and Mr. Long-ears began putting up the hammocks. But he had not gone very far toward that work when he called out:

"Oh, I say, Nurse Jane! Did you get any hooks with these hammocks?"

"Hooks? What kind of hooks?" asked the muskrat lady. "Do you mean fish hooks?"

"No, I mean hammock hooks," answered Uncle Wiggily. "You see, on each end of a hammock is a rope and this rope, from either end, has to hang from a hook fastened to the side of the porch, so the hammock will swing to and fro. Did you get the hooks?"

"Why, no, I didn't," slowly spoke the muskrat lady, coming to the door of the kitchen with an oatmeal spoon in her paw. "I never thought of hooks."

"Never mind," kindly spoke Uncle Wiggily. "I'll get them after breakfast."

So, piling the hammocks neatly in a corner of the porch, Uncle Wiggily went into his hollow stump farm house and ate his breakfast.

"Now I'm off to the hardware store for the hooks," he said to Nurse Jane, as he came out with a toothpick in his paw. "Soon I'll have the hammocks swung up for you."

"You are very kind," said Nurse Jane.

"Pray, do not mention it," begged Uncle Wiggily, sort of extra polite, because it was such a nice day.

It did not take him long to hop on his red, white and blue striped rheumatism crutch over to the nail, or hardware store for the hammock things. The iron man who waited on Uncle Wiggily gave him the hammock hooks and, carrying them under his paw, back the bunny gentleman started for his hollow stump.

Now, just about this time the bad old nose-punching baboon, the ear-scratching cat and the tail-pulling chimpanzee were having a meeting in the woods.

"How can we catch Uncle Wiggily?" they asked one another.

"I'll tell you how!" suddenly exclaimed a voice that came from a swamp of water near by.

"How?" all three asked.

"Let me try," was the answer.

"And who are you?"

"The hard-biting dog fish," came in reply. "I am a fish, but, being a dog fish, I can travel on land as well as swim in the water. Sometimes I live in a swamp like this. I'll catch Uncle Wiggily for you. Shall I try?"

"Yes!" cried the baboon, the chimp as I call him for short, and the cat. Out of the water came the dog fish, taking off his rubber boots, which he did not need on dry land. Off he started to catch Uncle Wiggily, and, having very sharp eyes, he soon saw the rabbit gentleman hopping across the fields of his farm with a bundle under his paw.

"I don't know what he has with him," said the dog fish to himself, "but whatever it is I'll bite it hard before I take him to those three animals, who will pinch his nose, pull his tail and scratch his ears."

The dog fish waited until Uncle Wiggily was quite close and then, jumping out from behind a tree, he cried:

"Ah, ha! I have you! I am the hard-biting dog fish and I'm going to take you to the cat, baboon and chimp. But before I do I'll just give a bite to what you have there."

Then, not stopping to ask what it was, the dog fish suddenly bit on the bundle the bunny carried, and, as there were hammock hooks in it, why of course, you know what happened.

"Oh, angle worms and lead sinkers!" cried the dog fish. "I'm hooked! I'm caught! There are four hooks in my mouth! I never thought I'd be caught by a hook on dry land. I'm going back to the swamp. They can catch Uncle Wiggily themselves."

Then dropping from his mouth the hammock hooks, which were too hard even for him to bite with comfort, away flopped the dog fish, and Uncle Wiggily was safe once more.

"What queer things do happen to me!" thought the bunny uncle, as he picked up the hooks and went on to put up the hammocks for Nurse Jane. "This was a lucky escape."

And I think so myself, and if the spool of thread doesn't unwind, and get all tangled up in the lawn mower when it goes out to play tennis on the grass with the croquet balls, I'll tell you next about Uncle Wiggily and the rats.

UNCLE WIGGILY AND THE RATS

"Well, well; this is queer!" exclaimed Uncle Wiggily Longears, the nice old rabbit gentleman, one day, as he walked out of his hollow stump farm house and stood in front of the corncrib. "This is very strange."

"What is?" asked Nurse Jane Fuzzy Wuzzy, the muskrat lady housekeeper, as she stood on the front stoop drying the breakfast dishes.

"Why, some one has been taking corn out of the crib," went on the bunny uncle.

"That's too bad," exclaimed Nurse Jane. "I hope they didn't wake it up."

"Wake who up?" asked the bunny gentleman.

"The corn," answered Nurse Jane. "You said it was asleep in the crib, and——"

"Oh, I didn't say it was *asleep*," spoke the bunny gentleman, with a laugh. "I just said it was in the corncrib. The crib for corn is not like the kind of crib a baby sleeps in. It is just a sort of shed with holes in the walls so the air can get through to dry the corn. But a lot of the corn that grew on my farm has been taken out of the

146

crib. I hope you didn't take it to make a corn meal pudding."

"Oh, not at all," cried Nurse Jane. "I only use the finely ground corn meal for pudding. The corn which you had in the crib was in ears, wasn't it?"

"Yes," said Uncle Wiggily, "it was, and a lot of the ears have been taken out. I wonder who could have done it?"

"Why don't you watch and find out?" asked Nurse Jane.

"I shall," Uncle Wiggily said, and that day he kept watch of his corncrib. It was not long before, as he hid behind the barn and peeked out he heard a noise near the crib. He peeked around the corner and saw a great big rat running away from the crib with an ear of corn in his mouth.

"Ah, ha!" cried the bunny uncle. "So it is you who have been taking my corn, is it? Hold on there. I want to talk to you."

The rat stopped and Uncle Wiggily hopped over.

"Why did you take my corn?" asked the bunny uncle.

"Because I was hungry," answered the rat.

"Hungry," exclaimed the bunny uncle.

"That's too bad. I didn't know that. So you really need some of my corn?"

"Of course, I do," answered the rat. "My wife and little ones have not had anything to eat in some time."

"Just you wait a minute," exclaimed Uncle Wiggily. He hopped over to the corn crib and opened the door, which was locked. Then he took out some nice yellow ears of corn.

"What are you going to do with them?" asked the rat.

"They are for you," said Uncle Wiggily, in his kindest voice. "Generally speaking, I don't care for rats in my corn crib. But as these are hard times, and as everything one eats costs so much, and as I have lots of corn, why, no matter what happens, you may have all the corn you want for your family. Help yourself."

"You are too kind," said the rat, and he was so surprised at some one being kind to him that he almost turned a somersault over the ear of corn he had taken out of Uncle Wiggily's crib without asking for it. Of course the rat did not know he had done wrong, never having had a chance to go to school when he was little.

"Now, don't forget," said Uncle Wiggily, as he hopped over the green fields of his farm to see how everything was growing, "any time you want any corn just help yourself. I guess we farmers are a little too severe with you rats and mice. We forget that even you may be hungry, sometimes, just as we are. So help yourself to the corn."

"You are too kind," said the rat. "If I were not so hungry now I would stop to thank you more properly. But, believe me, I am very thankful to you. I will take this corn to my hungry wife and little ones, and if I ever get a chance to do you a favor rest assured I shall do so. Hoping this will find you well I remain, Yours truly, Mr. Rat," and he talked just like a rich man having his stenographer make a letter on the typewriter.

"Pray think no more about it," spoke Uncle Wiggily. "And have all the corn you want." Then he went on and on over his farm to see how the things were growing. Nurse Jane asked him, next day, if he had caught the rats taking corn out of the crib.

"Don't worry about that," said the bunny uncle. "I'm going to let them take corn."

"What a queer rabbit he is," said Miss Fuzzy Wuzzy to herself. "Very queer, indeed, to let rats take his corn."

A few days after this the rabbit gentleman was out in his potato field to see how many weeds there were, when, all of a sudden, out popped the bad old circus elephant—not the good one—and the elephant, as he grabbed Uncle Wiggily cried through his trunk:

"Ah, ha! Now I have caught you. My friend, the blue-nosed baboon, asked me to catch you for him, and I've done it. Now you come along with me!"

"Oh, I don't want to," said Uncle Wiggily, sadly like.

"But you must!" said the elephant.

"No, he must not!" suddenly cried another voice. "You just let Uncle Wiggily alone."

"Who says so?" asked the elephant, saucy like.

"I do!" answered a bold voice. "I am the big corn-eating rat, and if you don't let my friend alone——"

"Ha! Say no more!" cried the elephant through his long rubbery-rubbery nose of a trunk. "I'll be good!" And then, as the rat ran out at him from under a hill of potatoes, the elephant skipped away so fast that he almost lost one of his trunk straps. For you know an elephant is almost as much afraid of a mouse, or a rat, as a lady is. I guess the big animal thinks the little mouse or rat might run up the holes in his trunk, as Hickory Dickory Dock once ran up the clock.

So the corn-eating rat saved Uncle Wiggily

from the elephant, you see, which was a big favor, I think, and the bunny gentleman was very thankful.

So this teaches us we may all do something good in the world, and if the Jack-in-the-box doesn't hop out to go to the moving pictures with the rubber ball, I'll tell you next about Uncle Wiggily and the catnip.

STORY XXIX

UNCLE WIGGILY AND THE CATNIP

"Well, aren't you up pretty early in the morning?" asked Uncle Wiggily Longears, the rabbit gentleman, as he came out of his hollow stump farm house one day and saw Kittie Kat, the little kitten girl, standing near the front porch.

"Oh, I don't know. Not so very," she answered, while she curled her tail around in a circle to make a soft seat for the butterfly that was fluttering around the flowers after honey. "I'm going on an errand, you see, Uncle Wiggily."

"And errand!" exclaimed the old rabbit gentleman. "Where to, pray tell?"

"Oh, just over to where Peetie and Jackie Bow Wow, the little puppy dogs live," answered Kittie. "I want to get some of their dog biscuits. Mother didn't have time to make any bread today, so she thought Mrs. Bow Wow might lend her some biscuits. They're nearly as good."

"Every bit, I should say," spoke Uncle Wiggily. "Only, if kittie cats eat dog biscuit won't there be trouble?"

"Trouble? How?" asked Kittie, surprised like.

152

"I mean won't the dog biscuits growl and bark at the cats?"

"Oh, how funny you are!" laughed Kittie, making her eyes go sideways like an automobile in a slippery street. "Of course puppy cakes, or even dog biscuit, can't bark."

"Well, if a tree can can have a bark why can't a dog biscuit?" asked Uncle Wiggily, joking like.

"Well, they don't," said Kittie, and then, laughing to herself at funny Uncle Wiggily, she started on across the fields of the bunny uncle's farm toward the place where Jackie and Peetie Bow Wow lived in their kennel house.

"Wait a minute! I'm coming with you, Kittie," said Uncle Wiggily. "I have to go look and see that my onion bed has plenty of covers on, so that the pansy flowers won't catch cold."

So Mr. Longears went with Kittie Kat across the fields of his farm.

They had not gone very far before the little kitten girl began to snif and snuff the air, and a sort of happy look came over her face, just as it does on yours when you see a lollypop or an ice cream cone.

"What's the matter, Kitty?" asked Uncle Wiggily, as she began to hop, skip and jump across the green grass.

"Oh, isn't it just too nice for anything?"

meouwed Kittie. "Isn't it lovely! Oh, how good it smells! And how good it will taste!"

"What?" asked the bunny gentleman. "Your supper?"

"No, I'm talking about catnip," Kittie answered. "See, here is some growing in the fence corner of your farm. May I have a few leaves?"

"Why, of course, you may—all you want," spoke Uncle Wiggily. "But what is catnip? To me it looks like a weed, and, if it is, I'll have to pull it up."

"Oh, don't do that!" begged Kittie. "At least not until I get some to take home to my mother, Tommie and Joie. We kittens all just love catnip. It's as nice to us as carrots or lettuce leaves are to you rabbits, Uncle Wiggily. Oh, I must have a bit!"

So Kittie Kat took some of the green catnip leaves and chewed them. She rubbed her head against them, and she wanted to turn a somersault right into the bunch of catnip, but she remembered that she was getting to be quite a large cat girl now, and turning somersaults is only for little girls or tomboy ones.

But, anyhow, Kittie had a nice time with the catnip, and she went on to the Bow Wow house, while Uncle Wiggily skipped over to the onion and pansy beds.

"Queer things certainly do grow on my farm," thought the rabbit gentleman. "Fancy now, catnip! First I know peppermint drops and chocolate creams will be springing up!"

But he was glad Kittie Kat was made happy by the catnip, which all kittens seem to love more than they do candy. And Uncle Wiggily picked and took with him some of the soft green leaves.

"I'll show them to Nurse Jane Fuzzy Wuzzy," he said. "Maybe she could make a pudding sauce of them."

Well, Uncle Wiggily was walking along over his farm, seeing how nicely the things were growing, and he was carrying the catnip in his paw, when, all of a sudden, out from behind a bush something jumped, and a voice cried:

"Ah, ha! Now I have him! At last I have caught him just where I can carry him off to my den. Ah, ha!"

And there was the bad old ear-scratching cat again. But just as Uncle Wiggily thought the cat was going to jump on him, and maybe claw him, as well as scratch his ears, that cat just turned as kind and gentle as could be. She meouwed so very softly and rubbed against Uncle Wiggily, purring, so nicely, and then she began nibbling at the catnip the bunny gentleman had in his paw.

All at once he understood.

"This bad ear-scratching cat likes catnip as much as Kittie does," said Uncle Wiggily. "I'll just leave a bit here for her to roll about in and I can run safely home."

And that's what he did. As soon as the bit of catnip was on the ground the bad cat (who was made good all of a sudden) began to tumble all over it. And she liked the green leaves so much that she never even noticed the bunny.

So Mr. Longears got safely home, which shows you that catnip is good for something else than making tea for babies.

That night, for the first time in a long while, the ear-scratching cat didn't yowl and keep everybody awake. She went to sleep after eating the catnip and she forgot all about the rabbit gentleman.

And, if the stone lid doesn't shut down so tightly that the coffee pot can't find a place to hide when the tea strainer chases it off the timetable, I'll tell you next about Uncle Wiggily and the baked potatoes.

STORY XXX

UNCLE WIGGILY AND THE BAKED POTATOES

"Oh, Uncle Wiggily, will you come?" asked Sammie Littletail, the rabbit boy, one day, as he stood first on one paw and then on the other, in front of the hollow stump farm house where Mr. Longears, the rabbit gentleman, made his home. "Please come!" begged Sammie.

"And bring peanuts!" called Billie Bushytail, the toy squirrel.

"No, matches," put in his brother Johnnie, frisking his nose sideways. "Bring matches!"

"Potatoes would be better," spoke Billie Wagtail, the goat boy. "We already have the matches and peanuts, but of course we need Uncle Wiggily to see that the fire doesn't get so hot that it burns us."

"Well, well! What's all this about?" asked the bunny gentleman, as he came down off the front stoop and looked up at the sky to see if any clouds were going to fall on his tall silk hat. "What's going on?" he asked.

"We boys are going to build a fire out in the woods after supper," answered Sammie, "and we thought, maybe, if your rheumatism didn't hurt you too much, and if you didn't have to do any farm-chores, that you'd come with us and maybe—"

"Have an adventure," cried Billie the squirrel boy, sort of excited like, as he interrupted Sammie.

"That I will, and right gladly," said Uncle Wiggily. "When is the fire going to be made, and where?"

"Right after supper," said the goat chap, "and the place is in the woods near the hollow stump school."

"Don't make it too near," said Uncle Wiggily. "If the school should catch fire and burn down you would have no place to go to say your lessons to the nice lady mouse teacher. And I guess you'd feel badly about that."

"We'd feel badly for the teacher," said the rabbit boy with a laugh, "but as for the school— well, worse things might happen."

"Oh, you mustn't talk that way," Uncle Wiggily said. "But—well, never mind," and he had to turn his pink nose away because it twinkled so it made him want to laugh.

"Well, don't forget," called Jackie Bow Wow, the puppy dog boy, who was with the other animal chaps. "Be in yonder wood as the moon rises, and we shall see—"

"The roast potatoes!" cried Jackie's brother, just like a phonograph speaking in a moving picture show.

"All right, I'll be there," Uncle Wiggily promised. Then he went back in the house to read the paper. After supper, thinking what a good time he would have with the animal boys, playing around a fire out in the woods, the rabbit gentleman went down cellar.

"Where in the world are you going?" asked Nurse Jane Fuzzy Wuzzy, the muskrat lady housekeeper, as she finished drying the supper dishes.

"After some potatoes," answered Uncle Wiggily, his voice climbing up the cellar stairs.

"How silly!" exclaimed Nurse Jane. "I don't need any until lunch time tomorrow."

"I was getting them for myself, not for lunch," said Uncle Wiggily, sort of shy like and bashful. "I'm going off in the woods with the animal boys to have a sort of picnic bonfire, and we're going to roast potatoes and—"

"Stuff and nonsense!" exclaimed Nurse Jane. "Will you never grow up, Uncle Wiggily, and act like other rabbit men? Of course you're nice, and all that, but you are getting too old for such silly things."

"One can never get too old to have a good

time," spoke the bunny uncle. "If you don't mind, Nurse Jane, I'll get the potatoes to roast."

"Well, I never did see anything like him in all my born days," said the muskrat lady as the bunny went down cellar.

Still she knew that Uncle Wiggily often did queer things, so she did not think so much about it as you or I might have thought.

A little later the bunny uncle started out to have some fun. Off toward the woods he went, carrying an empty milk bottle with lightning bugs in it for a lantern, as it was quite dark.

It did not take Uncle Wiggily long to get to the place in the woods where the animal boys were. They had gathered a pile of chips to make a fire, and Sammie, the rabbit, had brought the matches, while Neddie Stubtail, the bear boy, carried some peanuts. Uncle Wiggily had the potatoes of course.

"Now for some fun!" he cried, as he lighted the fire, and when it was burning nicely, with plenty of red, hot coals, or embers, the bunny gentleman put in the potatoes.

"When they are roasted we'll sprinkle salt on them, and eat them," he said, and all the animal boys declared that this was the most jolly time they had ever known.

Soon some of the potatoes were roasted, or

baked, in the fire, and Uncle Wiggily, poking them out with a stick, so as not to burn his paws, said:

"Now, boys, eat all you like, but not too much. This is real jolly, but, at the same time, I wish an adventure would happen to me."

"Perhaps one will," said Sammie, hopeful like.

"I hardly think so," spoke the rabbit gentleman. "It is now getting rather late, and will soon be time for us to go home. There are no adventures here, I fear. But if—"

Just then, all at once, before you could jump over a lollypop stick—that is supposing that you wanted to do that—a voice cried out:

"Oh, how cold I am! Oh how I shiver! I'm afraid I'll never be warm again, and I have so far to go before I get home. Oh dear!"

"Ha! That sounds like trouble," Uncle Wiggily said, and his eyes twinkled as did also his pink nose. For if there was one thing the bunny uncle liked more than another it was to help those in trouble.

"What is the matter?" asked the bunny. "Who are you?"

"I am the hand organ monkey," was the answer. "I am on my way home in my automobile, after having played the organ, and taken in pennies all day. But it is so cold that I can not hold

the steering wheel.   And if I don't hold it, and
steer right, I'll run into a lamp post, or something
like that, and hurt myself or somebody.   Oh how
cold my paws are!   Burr-r-r-r-r!" and the monkey
shivered like a drum stick playing a tattoo—rub-
a-dub time.

It was quite cold that night, but Uncle Wiggily and the animal boys, being so near the fire,
did not notice it.

"We might let the hand organ monkey take
our bon-fire and get warm," said Sammie, speaking kindly.

"No, it would only burn his auto," spoke Uncle
Wiggily.   "One moment, I have it!   I'll let him
take some of the hot baked potatoes.   He can tie
them on the steering wheel of his automobile,
and they will keep his paws nice and warm."

"Oh fine!" chattered the monkey, his teeth
jingling in the cold.   "They will be the best ever."

So Uncle Wiggily poked some more hot potatoes out of the fire and fastened them to the monkey's automobile.   Then the hand organ chap
could steer himself home and his paws were as
warm as the red cheeks of the wax doll, than
which there is nothing more warm.

So the monkey was able to get home without
freezing and when he did get there he ate the
baked potatoes.   Which shows you that some

things are good for doing two tricks. And Uncle Wiggily and the animal boys had a fine time.

So if the chewing gum doesn't stay out after dark, and get stuck on the letter box so it can't go to the moving pictures with the ice cream cone, I'll tell you next about Uncle Wiggily and the spiced pears.

STORY XXXI

UNCLE WIGGILY AND THE SPICED PEARS

"Well, this is going to be my busy day," said Nurse Jane Fuzzy Wuzzy, the muskrat lady housekeeper for Uncle Wiggily Longears, as she came into the dining room from the kitchen of the hollow stump farm house one morning.

"My dear Nurse Jane!" said the bunny uncle, with a polite bow, " all your days seem to be busy ones."

"I suppose you mean to say something nice," went on Nurse Jane, "but, as a matter of fact (as they say when they are telling a fairy story) I am going to be especially busy today."

"What doing?" asked Uncle Wiggily. "Are you going to iron the clothes or dust the piano?"

"Neither one," answered Nurse Jane. "I am going to make some spiced pears, and I was wondering if you would not help me?"

"Right gladly will I do so," said the rabbit gentleman, "but I don't understand the first thing in the world about spiced pears—except, perhaps, how to eat them or how to grow them on my farm."

"That is something, anyhow," the muskrat

lady said. "But, before you can eat spiced pears, they must first be made. Now I know how to make them. I will take some of the pears that grow on the trees in your orchard, peel off the skins, boil the pears in sugar, spice and other things nice, and put them in cans. Then they'll be ready to eat."

"Very good, Janie," said Uncle Wiggily friendly like. "But what do you want me to do?"

"Get me the spices, if you please," answered the muskrat lady. "I need some cinnamon, cloves, nutmeg and mace. All those will make the pears so much nicer. And as I shall be very busy peeling them, I will hardly have time to go to the store and get—"

"Oh, I'll get the spices for you!" quickly offered the bunny uncle. "It will be a great pleasure for me."

"I don't like to trouble you," said Nurse Jane.

"No trouble at all!" laughed the bunny uncle. "I may have an adventure, and that will be fun. Here I go—whoop!"

Away he went, leaning on his red, white and blue rheumatism crutch that was colored like a barber pole. Nurse Jane, who had gnawed the crutch out of a cornstalk, shook her tail.

"That Uncle Wiggily rabbit will never grow up—never," she said. "He'll always be like that—boyish. Well, maybe it is better so. I only hope he doesn't stop to play marbles with the nutmegs and sprinkle the cinnamon on somebody's hot cross buns, for I need the spices for the pears."

On and on went Uncle Wiggily, the nice rabbit gentleman: over the fields and through the woods to the spice store. There he bought the cinnamon, cloves, nutmeg, mace and other things that Nurse Jane needed. He put them, wrapped in paper, into his pocket.

"Oh, but those spiced pears will be nice!" he said to himself, as he hopped on toward his hollow stump farm house. He had not gone very far before he met Mr. Whitewash, the polar bear gentleman.

"Good morning, Mr. Whitewash," said Uncle Wiggily. "I hope I see you well today."

"Very well," answered the white bear, "and you?"

"Never better!" laughed Uncle Wiggily. "Let's walk on together and maybe we shall find an adventure."

"Fine!" cried Mr. Whitewash, and on he went through the woods with Uncle Wiggily. They had not gone very far before they met Grandfather Goosey Gander the goose gentleman.

"Oh, but I am glad to see you!" Grandpa

Goosey Gander quacked.   "I was feeling lonesome, and wondering where all my friends were."

"Come along with us and be happy," invited Uncle Wiggily.

"Yes do," added Mr. Whitewash. "We may all have an adventure together."

"All right, I will," said Grandpa Goosey, and he did. The three friends had not gone far before they met Uncle Butter, the goat gentleman.

"Well, this is a pleasure!" he bleated. "I did not expect to meet so many of my friends today. Come, I will treat you to some hot baked ice cream cones, as it is quite cool."

So the four friends started for the ice cream cone store but just as they were going down a little hill that led to it, all of a sudden Uncle Wiggily's hind paws slipped and he fell down.

And he accidentally knocked down Grandpa Goosey, and Grandpa Goosey, not meaning to do so toppled over Uncle Butter and Uncle Butter butted into Mr. Whitewash, the polar bear gentleman, and all four went down in a heap.

And then all of a sudden, they all began to sneeze:

"Aker-choo—ker snitzio!" sneezed Uncle Wiggily.

"Ker-fozzilum gittzio!" sneezed Uncle Butter.

"Washko-uggi-p o z z a z i u m!" sneezed Mr. Whitewash.

"Ichity - slambo - murkuzzio - gush!" sneezed Grandpa Goosey.

"Oh, this is dreadful!" went on the white bear gentleman, holding his nose in his handkerchief.

"I should so say," spoke Uncle Butter backwards. "We must be catching dreadful colds. Ker-chooly-choo!"

"And Nurse Jane told me to be sure and keep out of drafts," added Uncle Wiggily sniffling and snuffling. "Oh, dear! This is quite too bad—a-ker-cheezium!" and he sneezed again.

"What had we bedder do?" asked Grandpa Goosey, speaking through his yellow nose bill. "I dever gaught gold as quigly as this before."

"We had bedder go see a doctor I thinkd," said Mr. Whitewash, also speaking through his nose. "If we let this cold go—"

"I only wish I gould let bine go," Uncle Wiggily said.

"Speaking of doctors, here gomes one dow," cried Grandpa Goosey. "I say, Dr. Possum!" he called. "Gome and bake our golds bedder."

Up came the animal doctor, but, no sooner had he gotten near the animal gentlemen than he, too, began sneezing.

"A-woo! Whoo-oop! Zee-zo!" he sneezed.

"Why, even Dr. Possum is gatching gold," cried Uncle Wiggily. "There must be something very funny around here."

"There is," said Dr. Possum, sniffling the air and looking at the rabbit gentleman. "Where did all those spices come from?" and he pointed to a broken paper on the ground near where the bunny gentleman had fallen down.

"Why-why-they came out of my bocket," said Uncle Wiggily. "I got them for Nurse Jane to bake spiced pears—"

"And, instead, they made spiced sneezes" laughed Dr. Possum. "I see how it happened. When you fell down the nutmeg, the cloves, the cinnamon and mace scattered all about in the air. The fine spice dust got up your noses and you just had to sneeze. I had to myself. A-ker-cheezio-zut!"

"Ha! That is too bad, but we will soon stop it," said Uncle Wiggily. Then he gathered up the spices and put them back in the paper in his pocket, and nobody sneezed again, or talked through their noses, except Nurse Jane when she made the spiced pears. But she was used to that, so she did not mind.

And so neither Uncle Wiggily nor any of his friends had colds. I'm glad to say, and, if the loaf of bread doesn't turn into a cake, and try to

get into the rag doll's birthday party without a
ticket, I'll tell you next about Uncle Wiggily and
The Little Pond.

STORY XXXII

UNCLE WIGGILY AND THE LITTLE POND

Uncle Wiggily Longears, the bunny rabbit gentleman, was hopping along through Woodland near the Orange Ice Mountains, not far from Asbury Grove, where he had built his hollow stump bungalow. Mr. Longears was looking first on one side of the path and then on the other with his pink, twinkling nose.

I mean Uncle Wiggily had his pink nose with him; I don't mean he was looking with it. Gracious, no! He looked with his eyes.

"Hello, Uncle Wiggily! Are you looking for an adventure?" asked Johnnie Bushytail, the squirrel boy, as he scampered up a hickory tree to see if any nuts were growing yet. But it was too early.

"No, I'm not exactly looking for an adventure," spoke the bunny gentleman. "I want to find Baby Bunty, the little rabbit girl who used to live in a hollow stump."

"Do you want her to chase you and play tag?" asked Johnnie.

"Indeed, I do not!" cried Uncle Wiggily. "Baby Bunty is too lively for me! She says she

171

makes me chase her so I won't get old and stiff.
But it's fun to be sort of restful like once in a
while.   Now I'm looking for Baby Bunty
because Nurse Jane wants her to come and
have her paws and face washed for supper.
Have you seen her?"

"Do you mean Nurse Jane or Baby Bunty?"
asked the squirrel boy, sort of joking like and
comical.

"Baby Bunty, of course!" answered Uncle
Wiggily.   "I know where Nurse Jane is.   She's
baking a strawberry longcake in my hollow
stump bungalow.   But if you haven't seen Baby
Bunty I must hop along and look in other
places."

So Uncle Wiggily hopped along, and pretty
soon he came to the shore of a large pond.   On
one bank of the pond were growing a number
of tall plants, with thick, green leaves.

"Ha!   Those are nice plants," said Uncle
Wiggily.   "Perhaps they may have seen Baby
Bunty pass this way."

So, understanding the language of flowers,
which is about the same as that which is talked
by the leaves and vines, Uncle Wiggily asked
the green plants if they had seen the little rabbit girl.

"No," answered one large plant, "we haven't
seen Baby Bunty.   "We have been so busy try-

ing to shake off a lot of bad, red, biting bugs,
on our stalks and leaves, that we haven't had a
chance to look for any one. We wish we could
drive the bugs away."

"I can do that," kindly offered Uncle Wiggily. "I will drive away the red bugs that are
biting your thick, green, glossy leaves. I'll
knock them off with my red, white and blue
striped rheumatism crutch."

"Please do!" begged the plants growing on
the edge of the big pond.

So Uncle Wiggily drove away the biting bugs
by tapping on the green, thick-leaved plants
with his crutch, and the plants thanked the rabbit gentleman very much.

"If we can ever do you or any of your friends
a favor we shall be glad to," they said.

Uncle Wiggily hardly thought a plant could
ever do you a favor, but just you wait and see.
On and on through the woods hopped the rabbit gentleman, until pretty soon he came to a
cute little shady dingly dell, and there was Baby
Bunty lying on the grass fast asleep. In one
paw was her wooden doll—Sarah Jane Sassafras
Ricepudding.

"Oh, Bunty! Wake up!" cried Uncle Wiggily. "Nurse Jane wants you to come home!
It's nearly supper time!"

Baby Bunty awakened with a start, rubbed

her eyes, and then, holding her doll, Matilda Arabella Flapdoodle, in one paw, the little rabbit girl took hold of Uncle Wiggily's coat tail and back to the hollow stump bungalow they started.

They had not gone very far, and they were hopping toward the big pond of water, when, all of a sudden, out from behind a stump popped the bad old Skuddlemagoon.

"Oh, ho! Now I have you!" cried the Skuddlemagoon.

Uncle Wiggily and Baby Bunty ran as fast as they could. So did the Skuddlemagoon. Pretty soon Uncle Wiggily and Baby Bunty came to the big pond.

"Oh, if only this pond were little now," sighed Uncle Wiggily, "we could jump across it."

"What good would that do?" asked Baby Bunty.

"Why, once on the other side, we would be safe from the Skuddlemagoon," answered Uncle Wiggily. "The policeman dog lives on the other side of this pond. But, as it is now, it is too big for us to jump across, and if we have to run all the way around it the bad chap may catch us."

And then, just as true as I'm telling you, all of a sudden the big pond began to shrink up. It shut its banks close together and became so little that Uncle Wiggily and Baby Bunty could easily jump across without getting wet.

All the way across the pond they jumped, and, when they were safe on the other side, the little pond suddenly stretched into a big one again and it was so large that the Skuddlema-goon couldn't jump over.

"Oh, we're safe, Uncle Wiggily!" cried Bunty. "We're safe! But what made the big pond get little and then grow big again?"

"I don't know," answered Mr. Longears.

Then some voices spoke: "We made the big pond get little for you," said the green stalks and leaves on the bank. "We shrank and also stretched the pond for you. We are rubber plants, you know, and rubber can stretch and shrink."

That's just how it happened. Weren't those stretchy rubber plants good to Baby Bunty and Mr. Longears? And if the bluebell flower doesn't ring so late in the morning that the alarm clock gets late for school, and can't have any sawdust candy for recess, I'll tell you next about Uncle Wiggily and the funny stump.

STORY XXXIII

UNCLE WIGGILY AND THE FUNNY STUMP

"Good-by, Uncle Wiggily! Good-by!" called Baby Bunty to Mr. Longears, the rabbit gentleman, one morning, as he stood on the front porch of his hollow stump bungalow.

"What's that? 'Good-by?' Why, you aren't going to leave me; are you?" cried Uncle Wiggily. "Are you going to leave me after I found you in the woods, and took care of you and—and all that!"

"Oh, but you say I make you chase me and play tag, and that I won't let you sit around and get stiff and old and all the like of that! I'd better go away," and really it looked as though Baby Bunty were going away, for she had a little bundle in one paw.

"Oh, don't go away!" begged Uncle Wiggily. "I don't mind chasing you, and I was only fooling about you making me get old and stiff."

"And I was only fooling about going away!" laughed Baby Bunty. "I'm only going to take my painting lesson from Mother Nature. She knows how to color the flowers red, blue and golden, and she is giving me painting lessons.

My paints are in this bundle. When I finish
learning how to make a blue sky turn pink I'll
come back to you."

"Please do!" cried Uncle Wiggily. "I shall
miss you."

"Then, in an hour or so, if you walk through
the woods you may meet me coming home from
my painting lesson," spoke Bunty.

"I will!" promised Uncle Wiggily. Then
Baby Bunty hopped on with her box of colors,
and Mr. Longears went to see Grandfather
Goosey Gander.

"What do you s'pose Baby Bunty can paint?"
asked Grandpa Goosey, when Uncle Wiggily
had told about the little rabbit girl learning how
to make a green leaf look red.

"I don't know what she can paint, but she is
a smart little thing," said Mr. Longears. "It
would be hard to find her equal if you hopped or
waddled for one whole day and part of another."

"I believe you!" quacked Grandpa Goosey
Gander.

Pretty soon it was time for Uncle Wiggily to
start hopping along the woodland path to meet
Baby Bunty, for soon she would be leaving
Mother Nature's studio, where the little rabbit
girl took her lessons.

"I must get Baby Bunty to give my red,
white and blue striped barber pole rheumatism

crutch a new coat of paint," thought Uncle Wiggily, as he hopped along. "And I wonder just where I shall meet her!"

All of a sudden he heard a joyful sound.

"Hi, there, Uncle Wiggily! Here I am! Whoop-de-doodle-woodle!" and along hopped Baby Bunty. There was a smudge of red paint of one ear, a dab of blue paint on her left paw and a dribble of yellow paint on her hair ribbon.

"I've been having my painting lessons," she said to Uncle Wiggily.

"I see you have!" he agreed, with a laugh. "Well, we'll hop home now, and see what Nurse Jane Fuzzy Wuzzy has for supper.

Uncle Wiggily and Baby Bunty were hopping along, when, all of a sudden, out from under a pile of dried grass jumped the bad old Magoosielum. The Magoosielum is worse than either the Pipsisewah or the Skuddlemagoon.

"Ah, ah! I'm in luck today!" cried the Magoosielum. "A rabbit gentleman and a rabbit girl! Let me see, whose souse shall I eat first? I guess I'll take yours, Uncle Wiggily."

With that the Magoolielum let go of Baby Bunty, well knowing she would not run away without Uncle Wiggily. Then the Magoosielum began looking at the rabbit gentleman's ears to see where the best place would be to begin eating souse. For that it what souse is—pickled ears of nice rabbits.

"Well, I'll take some left ear souse first," said the Magoosielum, and he was just starting to do this, and Uncle Wiggily didn't know what to do. The rabbit gentleman saw Baby Bunty open her paint box.

"That will not help any," sadly thought Uncle Wiggily. "The only thing that will drive away a Magoosielum is pineapple cheese, and Baby Bunty has none of that."

Then the bad animal stood in front of Uncle Wiggily picking out a good place to begin nibbling the souse, so Mr. Longears couldn't see what Bunty was doing with the paint box. All he could see was that she was near a funny, old, gnarled and fire-blackened stump.

But, all of a sudden, Baby Bunty cried:

"Look out now, you bad old Magoosielum. Look out, or my friend, the Snippy-Snappy, will get you!"

And, as true as I'm telling you, there stood what seemed to be a little, short, squatty animal, with a big red mouth, a green nose, one yellow eye and one pink eye, one brown cheek and one purple one, and his teeth. Oh, his teeth were all sorts of colors, some even being Skilligimink shade!

"Oh, wow! Oh, this is terrible!" howled the

bad Magoosielum. "Don't let that Snippy-Snappy get me! I won't hurt you, Uncle Wiggily!" And away ran the bad chap, not hurting Mr. Longear nor Bunty at all.

"But won't the Snippy-Snappy get my souse?" asked Mr. Longears, when he saw that the unpleasant creature was gone. "Aren't we in danger from the Snippy-Snappy?"

"Of course not!" laughed Bunty. "I just made the Snippy-Snappy on the outside of the funny old stump, with my colored paints. I painted the Snippy-Snappy, Uncle Wiggily, to scare the Magoosielum."

"And right well you scared him," spoke the bunny. "You surely are learning to paint, Bunty." And if the safety pin doesn't slide off the cushion and try to sprinkle soapsuds in the eye of the needle, I'll tell you next about Uncle Wiggily and the queer log.

STORY XXXIV

UNCLE WIGGILY AND THE QUEER LOG

"Where's Uncle Wiggily? Where's Uncle Wiggily?" asked Baby Bunty, the little rabbit girl, of Nurse Jane Fuzzy Wuzzy, one morning. "Where is he?"

"Why, Uncle Wiggily has gone to the store for me," answered the muskrat lady housekeeper of the hollow stump bungalow. "He has gone to get me some molasses!"

"Oh, dear!" sighed Baby Bunty, the little rabbit girl, who had been found in a hollow stump.

"Why, whatever is the matter?" asked Nurse Jane, who had a dab of flour on her nose. And whenever the muskrat lady had a dab of flour on her nose you could be sure that she was making a pie. "Don't you like molasses cake, Bunty?" Miss Fuzzy Wuzzy asked.

"Oh, yes! Have you any?" Baby Bunty wanted to know.

"I'll make one as soon as Uncle Wiggily comes backs with the jug of molasses," went on Nurse Jane. "But why did you say 'Oh, dear!' in such a doleful voice?"

"Because I wished Uncle Wiggily were here

to chase me, or play tag, or something! I'm so afraid he'll get old and stiff."

"Well, why don't you hop off in the woods and meet him?" asked Nurse Jane of the lively little rabbit girl Baby Bunty could hardly ever keep still. "If you go to meet him you'll see him hopping along with the molasses jug," went on the muskrat lady, "and then he'll chase you, or play tag or let you help him carry the sweet stuff I'm going to put in a cake."

"I'll do that," said Baby Bunty, and away she hopped with her rubber doll named Beatrice Ethelmore Lemonsqueezer.

As she was hopping through the woods to meet Uncle Wiggily, all of a sudden Baby Bunty heard, near a little spring of water, a sad voice crying:

"Oh, I'm so wet! Oh, if some one would only help me out of the water!"

"Some one is drowning!" said Baby Bunty. "I wonder if I could save them?"

On a bed of soft, green moss, she put her wax doll, Sarah Ann Belinda Washbasin, and hurried to the side of the little spring. There Baby Bunty saw a poor honey bee splashing in the water.

"I'll save you!" kindly said the little rabbit girl. With a long stick she fished the half-drowned bee out of the pool, and placed him on a leaf in the sun where his wings could dry.

"Thank you for saving me," buzzed the bee, when he had shaken off some of the water. "I shall be glad to do you a favor, if I may. Do you want me to make you some honey?"

"Oh, thank you, no; not now," answered Baby Bunty. "Uncle Wiggily is bringing home the molasses jug. But some other time we may want your honey."

"Any time you do I'll give you some," buzzed the bee. Then he flew away to look for more honey flowers. Baby Bunty was glad she had saved the bee, which a big dragon fly had knocked into the spring of water.

On and on through the woods hopped Baby Bunty, and pretty soon she saw Uncle Wiggily coming toward her, with the molasses jug on his paw.

"Oh, Uncle Wiggily!" cried the little rabbit girl. "I'm so glad I met you. Now I'll help you carry the molasses jug and when we get home you'll chase me, and play tag; won't you?"

"Oh, yes, I guess so," answered Mr. Longears.

"It will keep you from getting old and stiff, you know," said Baby Bunty sweetly, as she took hold of one side of the molasses jug.

She and Uncle Wiggily hopped on, but, all

of a sudden, out from behind a bush jumped the bad old fox.

"Oh, ho!" cried the fox. "This time I have you!"

He made a grab for Uncle Wiggily and Bunty, but they were too quick for him.

"Run, Bunty! Run!" cried Mr. Longears. And he ran and hopped, and so did Bunty, and they got away from the fox. But, alas, they dropped the molasses jug and they didn't dare stop to pick it up, or go back after it.

"Oh, dear! What shall I do?" sighed Uncle Wiggily. "I have lost the molasses and jug, and Nurse Jane will be so disappointed! Oh, dear!" and he sat down on a queer log, that had a hole in each end, and warts like a toad all over it.

"It is too bad," said Baby Bunty.

"What is too bad?" asked a gentle, little voice, and out of one end of the queer log flew the very same honey bee that Baby Bunty had saved from the spring. "What is too bad?" asked the bee.

"The fox chased us and I lost the molasses jug," said Uncle Wiggily.

"Oh, ho! Don't let that worry you!" buzzed the bee. "Inside this queer log I and many other bees have a lot of flower honey. It is as sweet as molasses, and I'll give you all you want.

Here, make a box of some white birch bark from this tree, and take Nurse Jane a lot of our honey."

"Oh, that will be just fine!" cried Uncle Wiggily. "Nurse Jane can make honey cakes!" And the muskrat lady did. So you see losing the molasses jug didn't so much matter after all. And if the man in the moon doesn't want to come and live in our house and make the lady bug move into the garage, I'll tell you next about—

But there! I am forgetting!

There is no room in this book for any more stories, as you can easily see for yourself, without me telling you. It will not hold another one.

So I'll have to make up another book, and in it I will tell you a lot more funny things the rabbit gentleman did and the adventures he had and I will call it "Uncle Wiggily's Travels."

Be sure to watch for it.

THE END